Life of Sin 2

Lock Down Publications and Ca$h
Presents
Life of Sin 2
A Novel by *T.J. & Jelissa*

Life of Sin 2

Lock Down Publications
P.O. Box 870494
Mesquite, Tx 75187

Visit our website @
www.lockdownpublications.com

Copyright 2019 by Life of Sin 2

Lock Down Publications
Like our page on Facebook: Lock Down Publications @
www.facebook.com/lockdownpublications.ldp
Cover design and layout by: **Dynasty Cover Me**
Book interior design by: **Shawn Walker**
Edited by: **Kierra Northington**

Stay Connected with Us!

Text **LOCKDOWN** to 22828 to stay up-to-date with new releases, sneak peaks, contests and more...

Thank you.

Submission Guideline.

Submit the first three chapters of your completed manuscript to ldpsubmissions@gmail.com, subject line: Your book's title. The manuscript must be in a .doc file and sent as an attachment. Document should be in Times New Roman, double spaced and in size 12 font. Also, provide your synopsis and full contact information. If sending multiple submissions, they must each be in a separate email.

Have a story but no way to send it electronically? You can still submit to LDP/Ca$h Presents. Send in the first three chapters, written or typed, of your completed manuscript to:

LDP: Submissions Dept
Po Box 870494
Mesquite, Tx 75187

DO NOT send original manuscript. Must be a duplicate.

Provide your synopsis and a cover letter containing your full contact information.

Thanks for considering LDP and Ca$h Presents.

T.J. & Jelissa

Chapter 1

Jade

Bomp. Bomp. Bomp. Bomp.

I sat straight up in the bed, with my eyes bucked wide open. I wondered who the hell could be beating on the door like they've lost their damn mind. I kicked the sheets off of my body and slipped into my capris. Threw the blouse back over my head, and made my way to the front door, taking one step at a time. "Who is it?" I asked, but not loud enough to be heard by the visitor. I ain't gon lie, part of me was afraid and paranoid. I was a bit worried.

Bentley had been gone no more than ten minutes before the knocks had sounded. He'd left me alone once again in the trap house to participate in a mission I'd begged him to not to take part in, though my pleas had fallen in deaf ears. I'd been so emotionally down about it, the only thing I could do was to curl up in the queen-sized bed and try my best to go to sleep.

I was tired of being left in the house, tired of being on the run from the law who set out to charge me with a crime I hadn't committed. Tired of having mixed emotions for a man that I felt would hurt me somewhere down the line, and most importantly, I was tired of my pleas falling on deaf ears.

It was hard for me to show I actually cared about Bentley and whenever I did, receiving the opposite reaction of what I was searching for felt like a slap in the face to me. But, at this juncture, he was all I had to depend on besides myself. I trusted him to a certain extent. After all of the things I witnessed my father take my mother through, along with me, to fully trust any man was nearly impossible for me. I played him close to my heart. Watched every move he made closely. His every word to me was placed under a microscope. No matter how I acted in his presence, he walked a thin line in my heart and soul.

Bomp. Bomp. Bomp. Bomp.

I took five steps closer to the door, my heart banging in my chest just as hard as the person beating from outside. On the first night I'd stayed here alone, I'd gotten visits from all types of weirdos looking for product. Product I didn't have and product that was no longer served out of this apartment. It had gotten so bad that one of the addicts had broken the back window and tried to climb into it. I shook off the jitters from that experience and took a deep breath. I had to get it together.

Bomp. Bomp. Bomp. Bomp.

Now I was five steps away. "Who is it? Who in the hell is beating on the door?"

The banging stopped and there was a muffled voice on the other side. She was saying something, but I couldn't hear her clearly. I walked up to the door and placed my eye at the peep hole, and saw a short, heavy-set woman, with long weave braids that were in need of maintenance. Her mouth was running a mile a minute. Yet, her words were impossible for me to make out. I frowned and thought, *maybe it's a heroin addict.*

I slipped the chain on the door and unlocked it, before pulling it open. "Hey lady, we don't move nothin' out of here no more. If you want something, you gon have to go upstairs and see Santana. He moved the trap."

Santana was Bentley's right-hand man. They'd been hussling together in the Red Hook Housing Projects out in Brooklyn, ever since they were lil kids. Bentley had left with Santana to jump on a mission that would gross him seventy-five thousand dollars. I didn't know all of the particulars, but I could tell it was a dangerous one by how Santana had shown up only a little while ago with his face all busted up.

She waved her hand through the air and acted as if she was out of breath. "N'all, baby." She stopped to breathe, hunched over and placed her hand on the door jamb. "I was just coming across a hundred and forty-third and Broadway. The police like twenty deep over there. They got vans and a paddy wagon. Dressed in all-black with masks and black gloves on. They're about to make their way over here. Tell Santana and Bentley they gotta get out of here now."

My antennas shot straight up at the mentioning of the police. "What do you mean they're on their way over here? How do you know?" I felt like I was getting ready to crap on myself. The last thing I needed was to be fooling around with a bunch of cops. Bentley had shown me the newspaper that had my picture inside. The local authorities were offering seventy-five hundred dollars to anyone that would turn me in, or give up information that would lead to my arrest. My mother was going hard on trying to pin my father's murder on me. I didn't know how any mother could do such a thing, but mine was and because she was, I was on the run for my life and freedom.

"Baby, I'm telling you what I know. For as long as I've been in Harlem, I've come to know how they operate real well. If they're setting up shop a few blocks over, then that means they're coming this way, and the only people over here doing anything worth the police getting all grouped up about is Santana and Bentley. They stay in some bullshit and only God knows what they've done this time. Now, I'm telling you, you better warn them and y'all get out of here. I got two warrants and I gotta go myself. I've done my part." She turned and jogged down the steps.

I closed the door behind her, feeling like I was about to lose my mind and looked around the place for Bentley's phone. Whenever he went on a mission, he made a habit to leave me with his phone. But, after searching high and low, his phone was nowhere to be found. This left me defeated. I didn't know how to get in contact with him, or what I should do next. I stood in the middle of the living room, confused and turning angry by the second. Confused because I was lost and didn't know what my next move should be, and angry because I told Bentley I had a bad feeling. That I felt deep down in my gut something bad was about to happen, but he refused to listen. Now there was a potential something was going to happen, and I was in no way prepared for it. I was seconds away from losing it.

I tiptoed through the living room, pulled back the thick blanket acting as a curtain and looked out of the window. The sunlight shined right into my eyes, momentarily blinding me. I shielded them by placing my hand under my forehead and gave my eyes a moment to adjust to the rays of the sun. Then looked out and saw what seemed like a hundred police officers, tracking down the block of 145th and Broadway. My eyes got as big as saucers. I snapped the curtain back closed after seeing them jog across the street with assault rifles in their hands. I felt deep in my heart that they were headed toward our building.

I rushed into the bedroom and threw on my Steve Maddens. I laced them, then added a light spring jacket that had a hood attached to it. I gathered about five hundred dollars in cash and made my way toward the back door. I opened it and tracked down the stairs, down to the main door that would release me into the backyard.

As soon as I placed my hand on the knob the lady from before opened her apartment door and stuck her head out. When she saw me, her eyes got big. "Girl, you scared the shit out of me! Did you tell them what I said?" she asked, with two plastic grocery bags in her hands.

I put my finger to my lips. "Shssh. They aren't here, but the police is on the block. I gotta get the hell out of here. I got warrants."

The lady laughed. "Shid, girl, you and me both. I was on my way out too before I saw you."

Twisting the knob to the door, I pulled it open just enough to peek out of it. I saw the coast was clear and sprinted across the yard. I would get as far away from 145th as I could, find a phone and call Bentley so he could come and get me. We needed to get out of Harlem. It was hot. The cops were onto us.

I ran across the backyard as fast as I could and got to an alley before I heard a loud voice. "Freeze! Jade Robinson, do not move or I will shoot you!"

I stopped and threw my hands in the air, feeling like I was about to throw up. I casually turned around to see who was giving me these orders. A tall officer, dressed in all black, with a helmet on his head, had on some much gear it looked like he was prepared for a riot of some sort. The window to his helmet had been pulled upward. It had been one of the ways I'd been able to identify he was indeed a male, that and the deepness of his voice. He aimed a .40 caliber hand pistol at me with an angry scowl on his face. "Jade! I will shoot you. Do not move."

My hands were as high as they could go. "I didn't do nothing. I didn't kill anybody. My mother is lying on me. Please. You gotta believe me."

"Jade Robinson! Get on the ground. Now! Get on the ground now or I will shoot!" He cocked the gun and peered over the top of it, with one eye opened and the other one closed.

"I ain't do nothin'." I started to walk backward. There was no way I prepared to go to anybody's jail, especially not for a crime I didn't commit.

"Jade! This is your last warning! Get down! Get down, now!"

I don't know what I was thinking or why I did it, but I took off running at full speed, just as two of his shots rang out back-to-back, knocking a chunk out of the wood of the garage beside me.

I ducked down and kept on running as fast as my legs would allow, across the alley and along the gangway of the apartment building. I threw two garbage cans to the ground in the back of that building, hoping to make the path harder for the cop pursuing me. I peeked over my shoulder occasionally to see where my pursuer was.

He was picking up speed like a track star, running with the gun in his right hand. "Freeze! Freeze, Jade. You're only making this harder on yourself! Stop or I'm going to shoot you!"

I sped up as fast as I could, missing Bentley and hating him for leaving me to endure this on my own. *Pow. Pow.* The bullets whizzed past my head as he took one shot after the next at me. Now I was in fear for my life. I felt this man was trying to kill me rather than apprehend me.

Pow. Pow.

I rushed onto a side street and ran across it. The block was packed with all kinds of people going about their day. When they saw the man chasing behind me, somebody yelled out, "Twelve! Twelve!" The whole block seemed to go crazy. They scattered every which way. I kept running, inside an apartment building right back out the back door and into the backyard with this super cop on my tail. My breathing became ragged. My chest hurt and my legs were growing weak. I was close to the alley when he fired.

Pow.

I felt something crash into my leg and knock me forward. I kept running when suddenly, my right leg gave out, causing me to stagger, before falling to my face in the alley. The pain was so intense that I couldn't help but to scream as loud as I could. I looked behind me and saw the shooter about twenty yards away, running full speed in my direction. I could literally feel my leg vibrating with blood pouring out of it. "Why? Why? Why?" I cried as he closed in on me.

When he got to my fallen body, he placed his knee into the small of my back and pulled my hair so hard. I didn't know which pain was worst, the one in my thigh or the one in my scalp, where the roots had been ripped from my head. He took my face and slammed it into the ground.

Bam.

"You stupid black bitch, I told you to stop running. I could kill you right here and nobody would care. You'd be just another nigger dead in the alley." He yanked on my hair, then slammed my face into the pavement again.

Bam.

Things began to get real dizzy. I could feel the blood rushing down my face from my split forehead. When he raised my head to do it again, I heard four loud pops and then I fainted.

T.J. & Jelissa

Chapter 2

Bentley

I saw Jade run across 144th Street with Twelve running behind her, and made Santana stop the car. As soon as he did, I jumped out of it with my forty in hand. Took the alley and ran down it, figuring I'd meet the pair before they could cross it. I'd already had my mind made up. I was willing to do whatever it took to ensure she got away. I didn't give a fuck what that meant. Jade was already in my heart and it was my job to protect her by any and all means. So imagine how my heart skipped a beat when I heard the gunshots and saw her fall in the alley. I took off running as fast as I could in her direction. I watched her struggle to get up. She screamed out in pain. Then he was on top of her, taking a handful of her hair and banging her face into the concrete. The sight was enough to infuriate me on a level that I've never been before. I picked up speed and closed the distance between myself and the pair.

I watched him force his knee into her back and take her by the hair, only to slam her face into the concrete again. Her face was bloody. There was a hole in her leg, and the sounds she emitted were heart wrenching for me. He flipped her over and yanked her right hand behind her back. He took a pair of cuffs and slapped them on her wrist. He placed his lips against her ear and was saying something I couldn't hear, but I could tell it was vile by the spit that flew out of his mouth as he said it.

I didn't want to think about the consequences. I didn't want to think about logic or what I should or shouldn't have done. All I saw was Jade stuck in a horrible position that only I could rescue her from. And I saw a man violating her. Abusing her in my sight and that wasn't about to fly. I upped the

.40, aimed and pulled the trigger four quick times, before I could stop myself.

Boom. Boom. Boom. Boom.

All four bullets hit him from the neck up, knocking him off of her. He fell onto his back shaking like a fish out of water. A big puddle of blood formed under him.

I rushed to Jade and fell to my knees. I sat my gun on the ground and pulled her up. "Baby. Baby. Say something, ma. Please, say anything," I begged, looking into her bloody face. It was already swelling up. That made me even angrier. I was supposed to have protected her. She was my responsibility, had been ever since I'd convinced her to follow me. So, to see her at her lowest point, laid out in an alley with her face swelling by the second was killing me. I leaned down and kissed her forehead. "My baby. Say somethin', goddess. Please."

Santana pulled up in the alley inside his red truck. Jumped out of it and looked down on us. "Yo, what the fuck, son? Yo, you popped a pig, kid?" He put both of his hands on his head and looked as if he was about to lose his mind.

I scooped Jade into my arms. "Open the back door, bruh. Come on, she gotta get to the hospital. Dude's bitch ass popped her in the thigh and bussed her grill all up and shit. I gotta get my baby some medical attention." I could hear multiple sirens in the distance. That worried me, but not more than seeing Jade in the current condition she was in. She'd yet to open her eyes, and there was so much blood all over her that I felt nauseous. I wish it was me instead of her.

"Yo, fuck shorty, Blood. Leave her ass here. We gotta get a move on. Twelve about to be everywhere. We can't risk taking that bitch along, bruh. You just smoked one of the Jakes, B." He jogged around to his driver's seat and got into his truck. "Let's roll!"

I held Jade in my arms. "Yo, open the back door, nigga! Now! Open the fuckin' back door so I can get her in, nigga. I ain't going nowhere without her." The sirens appeared to be getting closer. The puddle of blood got bigger and bigger under the man that did the damage to Jade. I wished I had emptied my entire clip inside of him. Hated him for hurting her and I had never left her alone to begin with.

Santana slammed his hands on the steering wheel and mugged me. "Fuck! This shit is stupid! When we start saving hoes?" he snapped, before jumping out of the truck and running to the back door and opening it for me.

I climbed into it, and slowly laid with my back against the right passenger's side door, with Jade cuddled into my arms. Moving her hair out of her face, kissing her forehead again, I urged, "Yo, this ain't no ho, man. Shorty way different from what we're used to dealing with. I gotta protect her. I owe her that. Take me to the hospital."

Santana jumped into the driver's seat and stormed out of the alley. The tires kicked up gravel as he sped away. "You getting soft on me, Bentley. Whatever happened to us fuckin' with nothing but flawless bitches? Bitches that can contribute to the cause? Shorty ain't a benefit to you or me. She got the law all over her ass. Ain't got no money. No job. What is the use?" he asked in disgust. He pulled out of the alley and onto 145th and Lenox. He took that to 7th Avenue and got on it, flying past a yellow light, looking into his rearview mirror.

"Santana, word is bond. Kid, yo, shut the fuck up. She messed up right now. She don't need to be hearing you talking t
hat dumb shit. Now, I say she ain't like them bum bitches we used to dealing wit. It's something special about her. That's just that. Nigga, get us to a hospital as fast as you can. She bleeding profusely."

He looked over his shoulder down to us. "She getting blood all over my floor and shit. Damn." He shook his head.

He was getting me more and more pissed off, because he was focusing in on the wrong things. "Santana, nigga, you trying my patience. Just get us to a hospital, and we'll take it from there. Stop nitpicking on every fucking thing. You sounding like an old hag right now. Straight up."

He bent another corner and got onto the highway, storming. "Fuck you, Kid. You know what I'm saying. Shit just been real crazy ever since you been fuckin' wit this broad. I can't help but to state the obvious. And we can't go to no regular hospital. They'll report her shooting, and get all of us popped. We gotta go somewhere where I'm plugged. My aunt work at this lil clinic over on Seventh Avenue. We can bring ol girl ass through the back door and go from there. But I'm letting you know now that I'ma drop y'all ass off and get ghost. Both of you muthafuckas are on fire."

I rubbed the side of Jade's face and rocked back and forth with her. She was shivering, and that worried me. The floor was thick with her blood. "Before you go anywhere, make sure you toss that seventy-five bands in a book bag. I gotta have all of mine." I mugged him through the rearview mirror.

He scoffed. "I thought you was too focused on that bitch. But, I guess some things are more important." He laughed at that and kept driving. "Don't worry. I got you. A deal is a deal. Let's just get her over to my aunt, so she can do her thing. It's kind of hard to be Captain Save-a-Ho if yo ho dies." This brought more laughs from him.

I shot daggers through the mirror and was seconds way from popping his ass. He had me that mad. So much so that I couldn't even think straight. I simply hugged up to Jade and held her close to my heart, rocking back and forth. "It's gone be okay, baby. It's goin' to be okay. I got you. I got you. Don't worry about nothin'."

***

An hour later, I sat back on the couch and watched from a distance as Santana's aunt, Brenda, removed the bullet from Jade's thigh and dropped it into a metal pan. She sterilized her wounds, before stitching her up as only a professional could. "I don't know what's going on in this world that the women and children can't even walk around without getting shot. This world is getting so, so cold. It hurts my heart," the short, thin, yellow sista said, doing her thing with precision. "Santana, I know you bet not be responsible for this," she scolded.

He stood on the side of her, sipping out of a bottle of pink lemonade Snapple. "You can't always expect the worst of me, Auntie. I ain't have nothing to do with this one. I was just a good Samaritan." He smiled and drank the rest of the juice.

"Mmm-huh. Yeah, I bet. It's a reason you brought her to me instead of the regular hospital, so I know something is up. So, what is it?"

"Nothin' is up. We just wanna make sure she fell into the right hands, and not have to worry about the law and all that crap. That's it. Now do your thing, TT, it's good. I'ma make sure I hit your hand for the work too. I got you."

She continued to sew Jade up. "Boy, if I wanted your money, I'd take it from you. I can't charge you for this. This baby needed my help." She continued sewing, humming to herself.

I sat on the couch, worried and wondering when Jade was going to wake up. Brenda had shot her up with a dose of morphine while she worked on her. I prayed that lessened the pain. I needed to see her open her eyes. I wanted to hear her tell me the story about what had taken place after me and Santana had left. Her face had completely swelled up by this point from the beating by the cop. Though she looked deformed, she still surpassed a dime to me. She made me want to run out and smoke the culprit that had done this to her all over again. How could he batter and abuse somebody so helpless? A woman at that?

"Bentley, you been sitting over there for a long time without saying nothing to me. Are you okay?" she asked, placing Ace bandages over Jade's new stitches.

I raised my head from between my legs and forced a smile. "Yo, I'm good, TT. The day's events just shocked me a lil bit. I'm tryna get my bearings. But, I see you looking all good and everything. You lucky you family." I flirted, not mentally there at all. I was thinking about Jade and the cop.

She blushed. "Ain't no blood in us, baby. Whenever you ready, I'll show you what you been missing. I've always had a li'l thing for your li'l handsome self. You can be my li'l secret." She looked over at me and licked her juicy lips.

"I appreciate you for stitching me up, but Bentley is spoken for," Jade said in a voice so hoarse that I could barely make out the words at first.

I jumped up and rushed to her side. "Jade. Baby, you woke?"

Brenda took two steps back. "Okay then. Speak up for your man, honey. Excuse me." She giggled.

I brushed Jade's hair out of her face and leaned down, kissing her succulent lips that were swollen because of her assault. Her right eye was black underneath, the left one purple. She still looked good to me, but her injuries vexed me. "Baby, you good?"

She winced in pain and shook her head. "No. My thigh is killing me as well as my face. And if you had to do what I think you did to get me away from that person, then we're in

20

big trouble." She pulled me down to her and kissed my lips hard. Winced again, and kept right on kissing me, holding my face with her eyes closed. It lasted for a full minute, before we broke apart breathing heavily. "Thank you for rescuing me, Bentley. He had me dead to wrongs. I think he was trying to kill me."

I frowned at her then looked over to Brenda so Jade could know that she was saying too much. But his aunt hushed me, grabbed the remote control and turned up the volume on the news. "What the hell done happened now?" At the bottom of the television screen, it read, "New York City police officer was gunned down today by two known fugitives." On the right side of the screen were both mine and Jade's pictures. My heart dropped into the lowest pit of my stomach. Brenda nearly broke her neck to look both me and Jade over.

I snatched the remote control from her hand and shut the television off. "Look, TT, it's not what you think. When I got to the scene, that dude was on top of Jade, beating her head in for no reason. He'd already shot her. It was ridiculous. They're trying to charge her with a crime that she didn't commit. Had I not did what I did; he would have killed her with no remorse. She ain't have nothing to do with nothing. It was all on me."

Brenda looked to say something, but Jade cut her off. "He's lying. I shot him. I shot him because he was tryin' to kill me. If I hadn't, he would have. Bentley didn't get there until minutes later. By that time, I'd fainted from the blood loss," she lied.

Brenda backed up. "What do you have me in the middle of, Santana? Why did you bring them here? Do you know what they're about to do to them over this man?"

Santana smacked his lips. "Hell yeah, I do, but I ain't have shit to do wit it. Yo, my mans needed a lift to the hospital and that's that. Far as everything else goes, I'm as clean as a whistle." He tossed me a glare, and shook his head.

His aunt looked from him to me, squinted her eyes and then backed away from Jade's bed, toward the door. "Look, there's no hard feelings, but I have to call the police. I could lose my license if I don't. Besides, I didn't know how deep this ran."

I was already helping Jade out the bed, tying the hospital gown sash tightly across her back. "Come on, baby, let's get out of here. Yo, Brenda, you ain't gotta call them peoples right away. At least let us make up some ground or something."

She twisted the knob on the door and ran out of it and down the hall. I could hear the slapping of her shoes. "I'm sorry, Bentley, but I can't get involved in that shit. I gotta call them right away!"

Santana was the next to ease into the hallway. "Bruh, you know it's love, but I gotta bounce. I'ma fuck wit you in a few days. I got yo bread, so don't even trip. We'll meet up in two days and I'll give it to you. That's my word."

Jade fell into my body and groaned. "Just go, Bentley. I'll figure everything out. Ain't no sense in you going down with me. I'ma just tell them I shot him. They're already trying to pin one bogus murder rap on me anyway. What's one more?" She limped. Tears rolled down her cheeks. Then she fell altogether. I caught her, and held her up.

Santana got into the hallway and hopped, broke into a full sprint out of the room and down the hallway of the clinic.

I struggled to bring Jade back to a standing point. The sound of her groaning in pain threatened to break me down like a fraction. Fuck, I should have stayed back and never left her alone. Seventy-five thousand dollars wasn't worth the pain I knew she was going through. "Baby, it's okay. Lean on me.

Just wrap your arm around my neck and put all of your weight on me, I got you."

She bent over and flopped her arm around my neck. "Please, Bentley. Just go. Just go. The law is going to be here in any second. I can't let you go down for this bull crap when I know you were protecting me. I gotta face this music on my own, or I will never be able to live with myself."

I slipped my fatigue jacket off and covered her with it. "Nonsense. I got you. We're in this together, but I am your protector. You just let me worry about the law. You simply focus on getting back healthy. I need you, Jade. I need you to be as strong as you can be, so we can get out of here. Come on."

As we were making our way into the hallway, Brenda came down with a security guard. She stopped and pointed at us. The big buff brother radioed something into his walkie talkie, then jogged in our direction. "Jade, baby, I need you to be strong for me and hold yourself up. Just lean against the wall for a second. Hold on."

Jade winced and leaned against the wall. I could see blood coming from the bandage on her right thigh. That made the hairs of my body stand on end. "Okay, Bentley. But, what are you going to do?" she asked, breathing heavy.

I ran at the security guard at full speed. By the time he was able to stop in his tracks, I met him head-on and picked him up, before slamming him to the ground as hard as I could. "Stay down, nigga. This ain't got shit to do wit you!"

He scrambled around on the floor and came to his knees, reaching out for me in a swiping fashion. "You son of a bitch." He went to take his billy club out of its holster.

Two hard blows to his face and a kick to the chest caused Brenda and two other nurses to start screaming at the top of their lungs, and him to fall straight out on his back with his eyes wide open, tongue hanging out of his mouth. The nurses rushed around him and knelt down to give him medical assistance. By the time his back-up showed up, I had Jade downstairs in the parking lot. Five minutes later, we were in a hot car driving past the police as they were driving into the clinic's lot.

Chapter 3

Jade

"Ma, we ain't gon be here long. I just wanted to stop in here to see if the water is at least working. It's been four days and ain't neither one of us had a shower yet. You're my baby and all, but those scents coming from you is starting to make me question our relationship," he joked.

I glared at him and slapped my hand in my hip. "Oh really? Says the man who's been putting deodorant on over his unwashed underarms, then got the nerve to want to be all hugged up on me all the time. I spend most of the times holding my breath and trying to not pop out a stitch. But, I still care about you though."

Now he looked offended. "Damn, that's how you feel?"

I closed my eyes and raised my hands at chest level. "Hey, judge not lest ye be judged. I'm not judging, I'm just saying."

He walked into my face and slid his arms around my waist, pulled me to him a bit aggressive, but lovingly in the same fashion. "Yo, I was just playing, ma. You know I'm feeling everything about you. Ain't no scents gon run me away. Besides, we're both smelling some type of way. This what the grind is all about. You hear me?"

I smiled. "Yeah, I do." I leaned forward and kissed his soft lips. He held me around the waist, pulling me into his muscular structure. His big arms were my safe haven, my barriers of protection. His hot breath was like a magic potion. Every time I felt him breathe, I felt a bit stronger.

I didn't know how I'd gotten here so fast, but Lord knows it felt so good to be here. Protected. Cared for. Admired. Never in my life had I felt any of those things. Who'd ever think I'd find that security in a project dope boy? A monster of a man? A Red Hook savage?

He licked all over my lips, then hugged me to him. "Jade, you know I got us, right? I mean, I ain't figured it all out yet, but when it's all said and done, I'ma get us up out of this sticky situation. We got the world against us right now. All we have is each other." He held my face in the both of his big hands and looked deep into my eyes. "I got you, baby. You hear me?"

I nodded, then smiled. I didn't know why exactly, but I believed him. I think I believed him and had faith in the words that came out of his mouth because so far, he'd gone above and beyond to show me he did in fact, have me. That he would hold me down when things got tough. The fact that he'd not even hesitate to waste one of New York City's Finest was enough to let me know he was serious about me. I mean, it didn't mean my guards weren't still up, but it gave me some sense of relief to know I could trust him to a certain extent, to have my back. To protect me as best he could.

We'd been waiting for Santana to meet up with him so he could drop off the seventy-five thousand dollars for four days. Every time Bentley contacted him to see what was good, Santana would come up with some new excuse. I was strongly starting to believe that Santana was spinning him. That he wasn't going to give up his portion of the money. I didn't know how they'd accrued the cash, but Bentley was dead set on getting his bread.

We'd stumbled upon the boarded-up apartment about ten minutes prior to Bentley checking to see if the water worked. There had been green boards over all of the windows, but one of them was loose. Bentley wound up pulling it off and climbing through the window, before coming around and letting me in through the side door. The apartment had a strong stench of piss and cigarettes. But, I was just thankful that we were able to make it out of the cold. It had just begun to snow heavily, and the added wind caused us hell.

I laid my head on Bentley's chest and allowed him to hold me for a little while longer. "Bentley, it's freezing in here. Even if the water is working, by the time we get out of the shower, we're going to have caught pneumonia." I heard the wind blow against the boards, rattling them.

He held me and kissed my forehead. "It's good, baby. You see, I'ma nail this board back up there. Then, I'ma go outside and grab one of those metal garbage cans, light a fire inside of it so we can stay warm through the night. Santana is out in D.C. and when he gets back, he gon have my scratch, and we gon jump on that Greyhound and get the hell out of New York. We can go wherever you wanna go, baby. As long as you're with me, it doesn't even matter where we go." He rubbed his cheek against mine and kissed my forehead again. "Come on, let's go get you all cleaned up." He took my hand and guided me into the bathroom.

The door to the bathroom was hanging on by one screw. It looked like it was set to fall in any second. Bentley moved it out of the way and tore it from the hinges. He laid it against the wall of the hallway and looked down to me with an angry look on his face. "I imagined that door falling off and hitting you. That pissed me off, Jade. I would lose my mind if anything else happened to you. Especially if I could prevent it." He looked into the bathroom and turned up his nose.

The floor was filthy. It looked like a bunch of people had been in and out of it tracking mud. There was a ripped shower curtain. Part of it still hung on the rings and the other part drug along the filthy floor. There were big cockroaches everywhere I looked. They scattered gingerly across the floor and all over the walls. The medicine cabinet was opened, and the mirror was cracked. The shelves behind it had collapsed. The toilet seat was up. There was dark yellow urine inside of it and two huge turds. This made the bathroom smell putrid. I gagged at the sight of them. Bentley came and closed the lid. Flushed it and shook his head, holding his nose. "What type of people use the bathroom and not flush?" he said out loud.

"I don't know, baby." I limped into his embrace. Suddenly, I was feeling uneasy. The conditions of the bathroom had me second guessing our whole staying there for a few days. There was no way I could even imagine washing my body in such a place. I glanced over and looked down into the tub and saw the white porcelain was all dark brown inside of it. There were black rings all around, and along the drain was a dark yellow. There appeared to be a thousand roaches having a party in there, the big kind at that. There were so many of them I could hear them communicating with one another. That spooked me. I took a step backwards and out of the bathroom. "Baby, I can't do that. It's absolutely disgusting in there. I wish I would have never left my jacket with the five hundred dollars in it back at the clinic. Then, we could have at least checked into a hotel for a few days. You know, until Santana decided to show up with your money."

Bentley stood at the tub looking into it. "Damn, this is gross as fuck. I can't have you standing in a bunch of roaches, ma. What type of man would that make me?" He shook his head.

"Bentley, you're good. It's not your fault, it's mine. Had I remembered the jacket on the way out, we wouldn't be forced to go through this mess. The blame falls solely on my shoulders."

He snapped out of his zone, turned and took ahold of my arms. "Nah, baby. This on Santana. Bruh supposed to been showed up. I think he might be trying to stick me for my paper, but I ain't letting that shit ride. It ain't just about me no more. I got you to think about and because I do, everything gotta be taken up to the next level. I gotta hold you down. If he don't show up soon, word is bond, I'ma go find that nigga and it's gon be real ugly." He moved my hair out of my face with his fingers. "That nigga hate that I'm cuffing you, Jade. He acting like it's making me weak or something, but that ain't got shit to do with him running me my cheese. Word up."

His chest heaved up and down. His nostrils were flared. His eyes were low and turned into slits. He looked as if he were in a faraway place.

"Bentley, just calm down. I'm pretty sure Santana has more respect for you than that. Maybe he's gotten sidetracked. He'll be back at you soon, baby. Until then, we'll figure things out for ourselves. How much money do you have on you?" I asked, placing my hand over his chest. His heart was thumping so hard that I wanted to tell him to have a seat. I worried about him passing out.

"Eight dollars. I ain't never been this broke. I left all of my scratch in Santana's truck. Fuck, I'm so stupid!" He stepped away from me and turned his back.

I slid my hands along his shoulder blades. "Okay baby, well let's use a portion of that to get some bleach or something. This sink doesn't look that bad. Maybe if we get some cleaning supplies, we could clean it out pretty good, then take some wash-ups. That tub ain't doing it for me though. Yuck."

"Baby, if we use it on cleaning supplies then what will you eat? I ain't necessarily worried about myself. I just wanna make sure you have something in your stomach." He took ahold of my waist again. Hugging me and holding me oh so close. I could smell the hint of his wavering cologne. It mixed with his natural odor. Intoxicated me. I felt a chill go down my spine and another one that settled in my kitty. That was happening more and more lately. Nearly every time he touched me, or I caught a whiff of him, it caused my body to call out for him. This time was no different. We had yet to go the distance sexually, but Bentley was sending me on a journey and I found myself craving him.

"Bentley, I'm not eating anything until you do. It's like you said, we're in this together."

The wind blew so hard that it knocked two boards off of the windows. I looked over my shoulder to see snow pouring in from the outside. I could hear the whistling of Mother Nature. She rocked the foundation of the house, and reminded us that not only was the world against him and me, but her as well. In a matter of minutes, the apartment was so cold I could feel my teeth chattering together, and I saw smoke when we talked. Even Bentley shook from the cold as he held me. Up under the jacket, all he'd worn was a wife beater. I felt sorry for him. I hated how he felt that everything was his fault. That had to be a horrible way to walk through life. It made me feel guilty. I knew that most of the things he did, he did them for me.

"Baby, don't worry. I'm about to go out and get the cleaning supplies, and you something to eat. I got this. Do you think you could chill until I get back?"

I started to panic. "Bentley, you don't even have a jacket. How are you going to go out there and do all of that? It looks like it's about to be a blizzard." I rubbed my hands over his chest to calm him. I couldn't imagine him leaving out into the winter storm. The thought terrified me. What if he never returned? What if he left me all alone? What would I do? Who would I find to ride beside me the way he had?

As hungry as I was, food wasn't that important to me. Not unless he was prepared to take me with him. And, by the way my thigh was screaming, I didn't think I could make it more than a block without having to take a breather and rest it. I was hoping we could just hold one another to fight the cold. I never could see myself admitting it to him, but I was in need of his arms, his embraces, his security that allowed for me to feel whole and safe. It was a foreign feeling to me, one that I cherished with apprehension.

"Yo, I gotta make it happen for you, Jade. I ain't trying to hear nothin'. This is what real men do. So, I'ma go out here and brave these elements and I'ma be back in a minute. I gotta get a move on before the storm get too bad." He walked back into the filthy living room, picked up the board that had fallen off of the window and put it back up there.

I wanted to beg him to stay, wanted to scream at the top of my lungs that I needed him. I was scared to stay in the abandoned duplex all alone. I feared he might not return. That something bad might happen. But, the woman in me wouldn't allow it. I had too much pride. Had been through way too much in life for me to be able to bow down and release my weaknesses publicly in that manner. So, I played the tough role and set myself up to endure being alone once again, and worried about him. "Okay, Bentley, well I'll be here until you return. Just please be careful. That's all I ask."

He snatched me into his embrace and kissed my lips with so much passion that my knees became weak. "I got this, baby. I'll be back in a jiffy."

I prayed he would be. As his arms came from around my body, I suddenly felt weak and extremely vulnerable. I wanted to once again beg him to take me with him, but instead I turned my back to him, and slid to the floor until my knees were up against my chest. It was getting so cold that my toes were starting to itch. That always happened right before they got really cold.

Chapter 4

Bentley

The whistling wind sounded loudly in my ears, as snow fell from the sky in big thickets. It was so white around me, that it looked as if I was walking around on a blank sheet of paper. I rubbed my arms for the thousandth time and hugged myself, thinking evil thoughts that involved me doing some pretty lethal things to Santana.

How could my mans treat me like a sucka? How could he run off wit my bread, after I'd held him down on a mission to get his shit back? I'd been calling him since the day of the clinic, sending multiple texts, and even trying to hit him up on Facebook and so far, I'd not received a response. He was either really jammed up, or simply trying to play me for a pussy. Either way, I wasn't having it. I would track his ass down and get what was owed to me. That money was needed. It would be the only way that me and Jade could escape New York. We had targets on our backs bigger than a helipad. Life had turned against us quick, and now it was time to make it happen until a window opened up for the both of us to climb through.

I got up to busy Seventh Avenue, waited until three cars drove past before I jogged across the street with my ears feeling like they were ready to fall off. My nose was just as bad. It felt like it was being seared. My lips were so numb that the snot dripped off them, and I didn't even know it was there until I tasted its salt. When I got on to the other side of the street, I jogged down the block, then turned it to a full-on sprint. I was trying to get warm. The wife beater did very little to protect me from the hatred of Mother Nature. So, I took things into my own hands, running as fast as I could until I was inside Walmart.

The heat enveloped me right away. I got some crazy looks from the cashiers at their registers, and even the security guard that stepped from the game room. He looked me up and down, before walking over to me. I'd just grabbed a basket fit for carrying a small amount of groceries.

"Sir, are you okay?" the older black man that had to be in his late fifties asked me. I sized him up right away. If it came down to it, I knew I could outrun him, or whoop his ass if I had too. It just depended on the situation.

"Yo, I'm good, Dunn. Why you ask me that?" The store appeared to be crowded this day. I saw a lot of women pushing their children around in carts while they grocery shopped. They cast furtive glances over at me and the guard.

He took off his hat and scratched his head. "Well, the reason I ask is because it's below zero outside, and you're standing here in a tank top and black fatigue pants with red paint all over them. We've been getting a lot of junkies in here today, trying to find an escape from the weather. Now, I'm not saying that you're one of them, but you can see why I'd think that, given the way you're dressed." He put his hat back on his head and gave me a peculiar look.

I was about to curse his ass out, had I not looked at the wall next to the front entrance and saw me and Jade's wanted picture. There were three separate copies of them, nine by elevens. "Nah, sir, I'm good. I'm parked right out front. Just thought I'd run inside and get back to the car before my baby mother get to driving me crazy. I pulled the eight dollars out of my pocket to show him I had some money on me.

This seemed to give him a bit of relief. He smiled. "Well, my apologies, young man. Go ahead and do your thing. I'll go and harass somebody else."

I grunted. "I was thinking the same thing."

The guard looked over just as two addict-looking people came into the store scratching themselves. One was a tall, dark-skinned man wearing a Newport shirt, shorts, and a pair of gold boots. The other man had on overalls, and a big yellow bomber jacket. He had a bottle of Cisco in his hand and a lit cigarette. The guard rushed over to the pair and got to arguing with them. As he was arguing with them, two females slid past the guard and nodded at the men. They had on jackets that were way too big for them.

Having grown up in Brooklyn, I was hip to all of the hussles. I knew these females were with the two men and that the men were creating a diversion so the females could do their thing. What their thing was I didn't know. But, the men had the attention of all of the cashiers and customers within viewing distance. Since they did, I decided to take advantage of the situation. I grabbed a shopping cart and got to going in and out of the aisles, filling it up. I could hear the argument between the guard and the men getting louder, a lot of profanity being used. One glance five aisles over and I saw the females were hitting the women's section hard. Tucking a bunch of clothes right under their way too big coats, going so fast that sweat was coming down the sides of their faces.

My cart was filled to the top with food. I hit up the cleaning section of the store, and then grabbed a few of those big Walmart bomber jackets. I sized one up for Jade and grabbed it, that and a bunch of bras and panties. Next were the outfits, as many as I could. My cart was so full that stuff was falling off of it.

"Oh, my God, they're hurting him! They're hitting him! Somebody call the police!" a lady yelled, ducking back into one of the produce aisles and grabbing and wrapping her arms around her daughter. The little girl was crying, telling her mother that she was scared because the men were beating up the policeman.

The females got all they could carry and headed for the front of the store. They slowly tried to ease past the ruckus, when one of the managers hollered out to them. "Hey, Roy, stop those girls. I just watched them rip us off," she yelled, running in the direction of the women.

The two men came together and pushed the guard as hard as they could. He fell backward into the gumball machine, and they took off running beside their women, laughing at the top of their lungs.

The manager helped him to get up, and I steered the cart toward the back of the store, and into the employee's break room. There were two females just coming out of it, smelling like heavy tobacco smoke. When they saw me and the cart, they froze in place.

"Look, I don't want no problems. My family starving. It's almost Christmas and we ain't got shit to eat. Y'all see how I'm dressed. All I wanna do is push this cart right out that back door over there and be on my way. Act like you never saw me. Please."

The bigger sista with the golden braids shrugged her shoulders. "Nigga, I don't care. Shid, they pay me minimum wage. I got two mouths to feed. I'm finna go get on this register and act like yo ass don't exist. Life is too short." She waved me off and walked past me, leaving behind a thin white girl, with rosy cheeks. I expected her to follow her friend. "Come on, girl."

The blonde picked up her cell phone. "I'm sorry, but I can't let you do this. You're going to have to pay for this like everybody else." She stayed to dial something on her phone.

I stepped forward and yanked it out her hand. Raised it over my head and threw it to the ground with all of my might, shattering it into a thousand pieces. "Bitch! Get the fuck out of here. Don't you realize that I know where you work? Are you willing to die over some shit that's insured? Huh?"

"Shid, I ain't," said the big girl before she took off running.

The white girl got into a karate stance. "I've been waiting for a reason to use what I've learned and what better opportunity than to take down a crook. Oh, you've fucked with the wrong somebody today, mister. I'm giving you until the count of three to leave that cart behind and get out of here, or your ass is toast. I'm not kidding either." She rolled her head around on her neck. "One, two..."

I shook my head and looked at this crazy bitch from the corners of my eyes, trying to see if she was serious. When I determined she was, I laughed to myself.

"Three. Your ass is mine." She jumped back and then forward, threw a kick. "Hi-yaw!"

I caught her right leg and swept the left one from under her. Before she hit the ground, I scooped her ass up and threw her light ass onto a pile of coats that hadn't been sorted yet. Then, I rushed out of the back exit and into the cold. The snow had managed to climb two inches. Pushing the cart was a bit difficult, but I managed.

***

When I got back inside of the abandoned duplex, Jade, was curled into a ball, sleeping with my fatigue jacket pulled over her head. I could hear her snoring lightly. Instead of waking her up, I stacked the food and clothes to one side of the house, grabbed the cleaning supplies, and commenced to cleaning like crazy, all the way into the wee hours of the night. By the time she woke up, the house was spotless and I was letting the bleach water drain out of the tub. The bathroom was so clean that I would have eaten off of the floor now.

Jade came from behind me and slid her small hands along my waist. "Baby, oh my God. What have you done? This looks like a whole new place."

I allowed the water to run on my hands. I was thankful it was warm. I didn't know how that could be. I wondered if anybody lived upstairs.

"Yeah, I came in and saw you sleeping all good and shit and decided to not mess wit you. I knew I was gon get everything up to par right away. I gotta do the small things for us first, Jade, then that'll leave way for the big ones. I'ma hold us down. Just roll wit me."

She kissed my cheek. "I'm rolling, baby. I'm rolling with you one hundred percent. Can't you see me shivering like crazy, just like you are?" she joked.

I dried my hands on one of the towels from Walmart and stood up. "I got you a better coat for you too. It's thicker and bigger, just a Walmart special is the only problem."

She sucked her teeth. "Ain't nothing wrong wit Walmart. Ever since I been alive, it's the only place my parents have shopped, and I'm perfectly fine." She kissed my cheek. "We weren't blessed to be rocking all that designer stuff. I wish we were, but it's all good." She looked over my shoulder into the tub. "How does the water feel? Is it too cold for me to get into?"

"It's straight. I think there might be some residents upstairs whose heat is still on and that's a plug, because we're piggy backing off of their hot water heater. So, if I was you, I'd come on. I got you a bunch of underwear and stuff too. A couple 'fits. You should be good to go." I brushed past her and stepped into the hallway.

38

I still didn't like the fact that all I could come up with was cheap Walmart clothes, but they'd have to suffice. Once I got my money back right, I'd make sure that Jade was well taken care of. I knew she was a queen and it was in my best interest to treat her as such. She'd been through a lot, and we were both in a position where we couldn't depend on anybody other than ourselves. With that being the case, as the man, I felt the burden fell on me the heaviest. I couldn't let us fail or go without. The fact that Santana was playing wit my bread one way or the other, had me so heated that I'd had reoccurring visions of smoking him. He was my mans, but my money was a whole separate issue. Growing up in the Red Hook Houses, I'd seen niggas stank they own family members for less than a few gees. This was seventy-five thousand. Life changing money for anybody from the hood, especially me and Jade, and it was my money.

Jade walked into the hallway and grabbed my wrist. I'd been on my way to grab the clothes for her I'd snatched up. "Bentley, I don't know how you wound up coming up on all of this stuff, but I do wanna let you know I appreciate you. You didn't have to go out there and do what you did, especially in just a wife beater. It means a lot to me. That, the cleaning, and everything else you've done. You're really something." She kissed my cheek and rubbed me there.

I turned around to face her, looked into her pretty brown eyes. "I appreciate you for saying that, but you really didn't have to. We're in this together. I'm used to grinding under all circumstances and making it happen. For you, there will be no difference. I know you've been through a lot, Jade, and we have a whole army of problems ahead of us, but I'm going to try my damnedest to make things as easy for you as I can. I'll be your shield." I pulled her into my arms again, and it was like time stood still. Every time I held her, it felt like all of our problems were nonexistent, that the only thing that mattered was our embrace. She just felt so perfect to me, and I'd never felt that way with anybody.

She tilted her chin upward, took ahold of the side of my face, and very softly kissed my lips. "Thank you, but you gotta let me do my part too. If we're in this together, then my place is to meet you halfway with everything. I'm not helpless. Do you hear me?" Her eyes searched mine.

I'd never had a woman say those things to me before. For as long as I could remember I'd been taking care of all of my mother's bills, and she'd never tried to stop me. Then, whenever I messed around with a lil female and I decided to be on my tricking shit, not once had any of them tried to stop me, or made it seem as if they wanted to meet me half way in the streets. I'd been around nothing but takers. It was all that I knew, so being with Jade was going to be more than an experience for me. It was like I'd told Santana, Jade was different.

I nodded. "Okay, baby. I'll do my best. But, I'm letting you know now that I go hard for those I care about. Don't expect anything less than that." I hugged her soft body to mine. "Aiight, gone in there. Let me go get your things. Are you gon let me wash your back?"

Chapter 5

Jade

Bentley dipped the washcloth into the bubble bath three times before pulling it out and running it across my back. The water was nice and hot. It was a change of pace from the atmosphere of the apartment. It felt as if we were outside, even though we were on the inside. It was so cold that I was afraid to get out of the tub. Just sitting up, I could feel the cool air brushing over my shoulders and back, well, the portion that wasn't underwater. Bentley had told me about his journey to Walmart. I found it both hilarious and a little alarming, especially at the part in the story where he said they had our pictures posted in the front of the stores so every shopper could see it. That worried me because he could have been detained by the authorities, had someone seen him.

"Bentley, can you please tell me how you managed to do all of that shoplifting, and had the presence of mind to grab a jug of this bubble bath stuff? Something is not right in your head," I joked, rolling my eyes.

He laughed. "Yo, every movie I ever saw with females in them, whenever they took a bath it was always full of bubbles, so I thought that was a mandatory. I knew we both needed to get clean, but I just wanted to make sure your bath was as normal as possible. I was hoping the bubbles would take your mind away from the condition of the tub, or what it had been before I did my thing cleaning it. Why, is there a problem?"

I shook my head. "Oh, no. This feels amazing. It's just that if that were me there, I would have never thought to grab a jug of this stuff. I would have frozen once the security guard stepped to me and been out of there. On top of that, seeing our pics would have really freaked me out to the third degree."

"That's why I'm here though. Because thinking when the heat is on is what I thrive off of." He ran the towel along my shoulders, dipped it and then did my neck and back, all over again.

There was silence in the room. I really didn't know what to say. I felt vulnerable because I was naked, wounded, and feeling some type of way about him washing my back. I could only imagine what was going through his mind, and since there was a need to break the silence, I felt I should ask. "Bentley, will you be honest with me for a second?"

He dipped the towel and ran it along my shoulders again. Wrung it out and set it on the rim of the tub. "You already know I will. What's good?"

The water in the tub was filled halfway, because I had my right leg resting out of the water and resting on the rim. I was trying to make sure the stitches weren't ruined. We didn't know when the next time was I'd be able to seek medical attention. It was imperative I preserved them for as long as I could. "Well, I know you're used to dating and messing with a bunch of different females. I can only imagine you did your thing on a regular basis, but ever since you and I have been together doing whatever this is, we haven't gotten down. How are you able to do that? And is there any resentment toward me because of this?"

He laughed. "I definitely wasn't expecting that question. The other one either." He sat on the floor and scooted back so we could look into each other's eyes. His shoulder was up against the bottom of the toilet. "Jade, I ain't gon even lie, it's been real hard. You fine as ever to me, and I been feeling you since high school. You got this real sexy way about yourself too that drives me crazy. I even dig the freckles peppered along your cheeks and nose. I can't stand it when you're walking around, then you'll stop abruptly and pop back on your legs. That gives me all I can take." He lowered her head and shook it. "I don't resent you. And the reason I'm able to do what I have so far is because I know what you've been through. You ain't like the average female I can go in on. If I move too fast with you, I run the potential of losing you. I ain't trying to do that. I'ma drive at the speed that is comfortable for you. I mean, I can't flex like it ain't killin' me, because it is. But, at the end of the day, I feel like you're worth it. Things will happen when they are supposed to." He looked off into the distance. "What made you ask me that?"

I shrugged my shoulders. "Just surprised you ain't made your move yet. I been waiting on it. I don't know what I'd do if you did, but I know we're both living on borrowed time. What if we never get the chance to be together? What if something happens, God forbid, and we're always in wonder of what it would have been like to be together? Then what?" I didn't know what I was getting at. All I knew was my body, my soul, and my heart was calling out for Bentley. I knew that in order for us to be together, there were risks that had to be taken. Risks that could take him away from me. I didn't want to go the rest of my life wondering what it would have been like to render all of myself to the first man that actually gave a damn about me. I desired Bentley. I wasn't entirely sure if I was all the way ready to go there with him. But, I was also wondering if I was willing to go my whole life not knowing him in that light.

He exhaled and came to his knees. "Jade, I'm ready whenever you are. You're all I see. The only person I care about outside of my mother. I would love to have you. Love to make love to that perfect body. I mean, at least we'd stay warm." He smiled and rubbed my cheek. "But, you sure you're ready for something like that?"

My body was calling. But, my mind was like a Rubik's Cube of emotions. I wanted to feel a deeper connection with him. I needed to lock him down so his eyes wouldn't wander to anyone outside of us. More than once during our four days travel, I'd caught him peeping this female or that one, and I knew it had a lot to do with his nature calling. I couldn't allow for anybody to swoop in and take him away, simply because my mind wasn't in total agreement with physical. Sacrifices had to be made, and I knew what I had to do. "Bentley, to be honest, I want you just as bad as you want me, if not more." I stretched the truth to appease the male nature inside of him.

His eyes lit up. "Yo, you serious, ma?"

I nodded. "Sure am. So, when do you want to do this?" I asked, with way more confidence than I felt. I was terrified, not only because of the emotional aspect of it all, but because unbeknownst to Bentley, I'd never been with a man before in my entire life.

He stood up, with bucked eyes. "Jade, don't play wit me. I been lusting over you since day one. The closest I've gotten just a small taste of you, and even that was good. But, I'm ready now." He took his beater off and dropped it to the floor, then went to undo his pants. His chest muscles flexed uncontrollably. I couldn't take my eyes off the ripples of his stomach muscles. They were defined as if all he did was sit-ups and crunches. When he dropped his pants to his ankles, he damn near tripped, trying to come out of them.

I busted up laughing. "Bentley. Baby, calm down. Why don't you get in the tub after me, and get clean? Then we'll make us some sandwiches, get full, and take it from there. There is no rush, baby. I ain't goin' nowhere, I promise." I motioned for him to come forward. When he did, I took his handsome face into my hands and kissed him soft at first, and then with so much passion that by the end of it, we were both breathing hard. My nipples grew hard. He dared to take ahold of my right breast, squeezing it. His thumb played over the areola, then pulled the nipple, sending a shiver down my spine. "Bentley. Baby," I gasped. He sucked the tip of my right breast into his mouth and trailed his tongue in circles around it, smacking loudly. "Jade, I want you so bad, ma. Word is bond, I'm crazy about you already. I don't what is wrong wit me, but I do." His lips wrapped around my left breast and pulled on the nipple before he stood up, his penis pressing against his boxers, pitching a tent. "Let's finish getting you clean, then you gotta unleash me. You gotta unleash this beast."

***

When he came out of the bathroom, I'd made the best pallet I could, using the two blankets he'd managed to grab from Walmart and our bomber jackets. It was so cold in the house that I was shaking like a bush blowing in the wind. Dressed in only a pair of panties and one of the bras he copped for me, I was freezing but ready for him, or as ready as I could get.

He stood shirtless at the end of the hallway, acting as if the cold was only a figment of my imagination. His body was muscled out and flawless to me. I found myself getting shy, wondering if I'd measure up to his expectations. Every time I saw him in the projects, the females in front of him were always so gorgeous. They made me feel inferior, them and the verbal assassinations from my parents toward myself. I was thankful for the light that shined in through the window. It illuminated him but wasn't bright enough to out me under its glow. I'd strategically positioned the pallet so that he and I would be in utter darkness while we did our thing. I know that sounded crazy, being that he'd seen me naked in the tub and all but even still, my insecurities were getting the better of me.

"Let's do this, baby. I see you done hooked it up as best you could, huh?" He walked over and knelt beside me, straddled my waist as I laid back looking up at him terrified.

"Yeah. We gotta work wit what we got, right?" My hands slid along his shoulder blades. They were big, firm and full of heat. He smelled like body wash from the bathroom. Just him looming over me caused me to feel a bit warmer.

He nuzzled his face into the crook of my neck and kissed me there, then gently nibbled the same spot. "Baby, we can take it as slow as you want. Please tell me for the last time that you really wanna do this." He raised his face to look down at me. He rubbed my hair out of my face, then brushed my cold cheeks with the back of his fingers.

I took a moment to think about the importance of our union. Thought about losing him, and what it would feel like to have never gotten the chance to know him thoroughly, and my decision was made for me. "I'm ready, baby. Just be gentle."

He stared down at me. Then slowly, his head began to nod. His face went back to the crook of my neck. He sucked harder now and with more urgency. The tingles attacked me from all over. I found myself shaking and running my hands up and down his muscular back. He sucked a path along my neck that led downward. Planted kisses over my chest, then unhooked my bra, tossing it aside. He squeezed my breasts together with his big hands, before nursing on both nipples loudly.

The sound effects had me out of breath. I opened my thighs wider to accommodate his body. I felt his tongue roll circles around my areolas, then he was sucking them again with hunger, while his hand ran along my stomach, all the way down to the waistband of my panties. Once there his hand slipped inside, until he was rubbing all over my garden. My

46

heart skipped a beat. I couldn't believe this was happening. I wasn't ready. As much as I wanted him, I just wasn't ready for what would come next. His finger slipped between the folds of my valley. Then he pulled them out, only to smush my lips together.

"Damn, Jade. You strapped, baby. You so fuckin' strapped." He kissed down my stomach and pulled my panties down to my ankles and off. Opened my thighs and planted a kiss right on my cat. "Watch this, Jade."

I closed my eyes and tried as best I could to zone out with him. To be there sexually, but no matter how hard I tried, I couldn't stop my brain from racing. From thinking about the predicament, we were currently in, missing my sisters, to trying to understand how my mother could pin a murder that she'd committed on me. I thought about the fact that my first time with a man I actually cared about would be in an abandoned apartment, on a cold floor, and before I could stop myself, I sat up and scooted backwards. Bentley smacked loudly as he released my left sex lip from his mouth and sat back on his haunches.

"What's the matter, baby?"

I brought my knees to my chest, wrapping the bomber jacket around it. "I'm sorry, baby. I just can't slow my mind down. I'm missing my sisters. I'm worried about what's gonna happen to us pretty soon. We don't have any protection, and I don't want my first time to be on the floor of an abandoned apartment. I deserve more than this. I will understand if you're angry. I should have never agreed to go this far. I knew I wasn't ready."

He slid beside me and wrapped me into his arms. "Ma, it's good. Yo you're right. This my bad. I know damn well you deserve more than this. And baby, I didn't know it was your first time. Had I known that; I would have never attempted to make love to you here. Yo, I'm so, so sorry." He held me so tight I could barely breathe.

"I'm sorry too, Bentley. I should have told you everything before we got to this point. I mean, I want you just as bad, but it has to be under better conditions. Does that make sense to you?"

"Perfect sense, baby. I promise, we gon figure this out. Everything is looking a bit dark for us right now, but we will figure it out together. Do you hear me?" He planted a kiss on my forehead.

"Yes."

"Baby, don't ever do nothing with me that you don't want to. Please. Always keep you in mind before me. I'll be okay. In my mind, it'll always be about you. You got that?"

I held him tighter. "I don't know why that is, but yes, baby. I got it. Bentley?"

"Yeah, ma?"

"Do you mind just holding me tonight? It's so cold, and I just need to feel warm and safe. Please." I laid on my side.

"No doubt. I got you, baby. For always." He pulled me back into his chest and we snuggled up together. His lips were pressed against the back of my neck. "I'ma hold you down, Jade. I know everybody done hurt you, but I won't. I promise, ma. I'ma be that one to show you different."

I squeezed my eyes tight as the tears ran down my cheeks. Never had anyone spoke with so much passion and sincerity in regards to me. I didn't understand the level of care Bentley had for me. It was both comforting and scary. I didn't know how long it could possibly last if I didn't do my part for him. I silently prayed Jehovah would fix my brain. That he'd help me to meet Bentley halfway in a physical sense. "Bentley, before we drift off, I have one more question, and the only reason I'm going to ask you this is because we've never gotten any clarification on it. But, what are we to each other? Are we together? Or are we just two project kids fighting against all odds, taking it one day at a time, with no title? I need to know because I'm battling with so many emotions within myself in regards to us, and I don't even know if we're a couple. I'm so lost right now."

He held me tighter. "I'm yours, Jade. I ain't goin' nowhere away from you. You're my baby. That's how I feel. If you didn't know now you do."

Those words soothed my soul, caused me to shiver even worse than I already was. "Then, it's us. I'm yours, baby. "

T.J. & Jelissa

Chapter 6

Bentley

Santana hit me up three days later and we wound up meeting up at the abandoned apartment. I was so heated watching him get out of the money-green Lexus truck, with the mirror tints that by the time he stepped inside the apartment, and crossed the threshold, I couldn't control my temper anymore. I snatched his ass up and slammed him into the wall, putting a huge dent inside of it.

"Nigga, what the fuck, Bentley?" he exclaimed.

I had him jacked all the way up. The apartment was freezing. There was a storm going on outside, and it was so cold on the inside that my toes were frozen. "Nigga, I'ma ask you one time. Where the fuck is my money, Santana?" I tightened the grip I had on him.

He curled his lip and mugged me with mounting anger. "Bentley, I know you heated because a nigga been gon for a lil while, but on everything I love, if you don't let me down we about to tear this bitch up."

I lifted him even higher in the air. His Timbs were on their tiptoes. "Where the fuck my money at, nigga?" I was so heated my eyes were blurry. My heart pounded in my chest.

"Yo, I got yo shit in the truck, nigga. Fuck. Calm yo as down, Dunn." He placed his leather gloved hand on top of mine to loosen the grip.

Jade walked up and laid her hand on my shoulder. "Bentley, he say he got it. It's good. Let him down. That's ya mans, right?"

I started to shake. I kept seeing images of Santana in my mind with his head blown off, and me standing over him with the smoking gun. Wasn't no nigga gon beat me out of what was owed to me. I was a Red Hook nigga. Used to surviving under the gun and taking what I wanted, but never had anybody taken anything from me without meeting the Reaper. I had mad love for Santana, but I loved my money more, especially since me and Jade were in a serious jam. I released him and took a few steps away from him. "Blood, you knew we was in a fucked-up position and you took your time getting back at me. You ain't let me know nothin'! That's fuck shit!"

Jade walked out of the room and down the hallway. I don't know where she wound up, but clearly, she was trying to give me and Santana some room to talk. I knew that if my toes were frozen, hers were as well. I felt like a bum. What type of nigga couldn't keep his lady safe from harm?

Santana wiped his mouth, then fixed his leather jacket. "Yo, my word, you the only nigga I'll ever let get away with that shit. Don't nobody put they hands on me, B. Now, if you'll calm down, I'll tell you what happened."

I paced back and forth, fuming. I couldn't even look at that nigga. Every time I thought about looking into his face murder crossed my mind. "This shit better be good. Better be good enough to explain to me why you'd go on hiatus with my muthafuckin' cash, nigga. You coulda dropped my shit off and did ya own thing later. My word. Fuck!" I balled my fists, mugging his ass. My toes were getting colder and colder.

He took out the pink-colored Sprite mixed with lean from his coat pocket and turned it up. "Huh, nigga, take a shot of this shit." He handed it out to me.

I stepped forward and smacked that shit out of his hand so hard that the contents spilled all over him and me, and I didn't give no fucks. "I don't wanna drink. I want my bag, nigga!"

He held his arms out like a cross, with the pink Sprite dripping off of his nose and chin. "Yo! Bentley, on my Blood, nigga, you testing my patience." He wiped his face. "Nigga, I got jammed up down in Nebraska busting a move. That's why you ain't heard from me. My li'l bitch dropped fifteen bands to get me sprung. I touched down literally six hours ago. Got myself right then hit you right up. So calm ya ass down. You ain't the only mafucka wit problems."

He pulled out a Gucci handkerchief and cleaned himself up.

Jade waltzed back into the living room with her bomber jacket zipped all the way up. She also had the blanket wrapped around her. That infuriated me even more.

Santana took a blunt from his ear and sparked it. "Yo, y'all in this bitch trapping fa real. Why is it so cold in here?"

Both me and Jade shot daggers at him. "Yo, go get my cash, Santana, so I can get me and my baby right. I'm tired of seeing her suffer from this punk-ass cold. This ain't right."

He jerked his head back. "Yo baby?" Scoffed. "Nigga, this cold weather gotta be getting to yo head. Talking 'bout yo baby. This is us. We fuck wit bad bitches only. Always have. Strictly Spanish bitches and yella hoes, and even they don't get the baby title. No offense, shorty."

Jade smacked her lips. "I ain't gon take no offense to that because I ain't neither a bitch nor a ho. I'm a queen. Let's get that straight right now. Second of all, you heard what he said. *His* baby. That's all that needs to be said." She rolled her eyes, stepping beside me.

Santana frowned. "Bitch."

I pulled Jade behind me and stepped into his face. "This ain't that, bruh. On everything it ain't. Leave her out of this and focus on my muthafuckin' money. Where dat at?"

Santana mugged me for a while in silence. He kissed his teeth and nodded his head. "Yeah, aiight, bruh. Let's focus on that."

***

Two hours later, all three of us were standing in the hotel room of the Ramada Inn. Santana came and dropped the big duffle bag on the bed and unzipped it. He took out four stacks of money and placed them by the pillow. Then he pulled out two silver packages that had Chinese writing all over them. "Look, that's fifteen thousand in cash, and this is two bricks of that China White. Street value of a hundred and fifty thousand dollars."

I snatched the bags and rifled through it. There were five more bricks inside of it, but no more cash. "Yo, nigga, you sixty bands short. Where the fuck is the rest of my money?" I asked through clenched teeth.

He glanced over at me. "Nigga, I'm giving you two bricks and fifteen thousand dollars. That's a total of a hunnit and sixty-five racks. That's ninety extra gees you getting. What's really good?"

My blood pressure went through the roof. "Santana, I'm on the muthafuckin' run, nigga. Where the fuck am I gon be able to sit down and set up shop to buss down two birds? Where?"

"Bruh, we can fuck around in Jersey, or Nebraska. I got traps all over both places. You should have that one-fifty in a matter of weeks, if not sooner. Look, I needed to use that other cash for bail and to cop these chickens so I could make back what I had to trick off on getting sprung. You know how this shit go. In the game you're up one minute, and the next you're down. Luckily, we hit that other lick so I could break out and handle my bidness. Bentley, that China eighty-five percent, nigga. You could step on it again and wind up making three hunnit gees as long as you dime it up." He exhaled loudly and sat on the bed. "Nigga, I was fucked up, what you want from me?"

Jade and I made eye contact. She shook her head. "Bentley, can I talk to you for a minute in the bathroom please?" She walked into it and waited for me. I wanted to check that nigga Santana so bad, I knew I had to get out of the room before I said something that would have caused us to become mortal enemies. I was tired of his bullshit. So, I followed Jade into the bathroom and she closed the door behind us.

"Yeah, talk some sense into that angry-ass nigga, shorty. Word up," Santana yelled.

She ignored him and stepped into my face and kissed my lips. "Look, baby, I know you're vexed right now, but it's more than what we had. Instead of showing him your emotions, just take it as a lesson. Now, you see what type of friend you're dealing with. Just goes to show we really are all we have. As long as we know that, and keep that at the forefront of our minds, we'll be able to navigate around the bull crap and capitalize off of our trespassers." She held my face in her little hands again. I loved when she did that, for some reason. It was like this little woman was, in a way, pulling the reins on me. Keeping me calm and focused with just a simple gesture by the use of her soft hands. "You feel me?"

Her eyes gazed into mine. She gave me a serious, yet sexy ass stare that softened me. I melted, and the act of murdering Santana over my paper was pushed to the back of my mind for the moment. I didn't know how long it would stay there, because in my head, that nigga had gotten over on me. He'd taken away the cash I was owed and turned it into a product that would have to be sold in order for me to get my money. That was bullshit, and it would not go unpunished by me. He'd shattered more than a few elements of our friendship. I'd file the transgression away, then get up with his ass at a later time.

I took a deep breath, and exhaled, and stroked Jade's cheek. "Damn, baby, you're right. We were just in a freezing, abandoned apartment with eight dollars to our name. At least now we'll have a little breathing room, so we can move about a li'l bit. Gotta get you some warm clothes and boots for the winter. Maybe get that hair done and those nails. Fifteen gees a go a long way. Then after that, we'll cop a bus ticket and leave New York. Just roll until we come to a new place. Start over. Maybe get new names and everything. Them Latinos do it all the time, so why can't we?"

She looked into my eyes, then hugged me. She laid her head on my chest. "We can, baby. We can go anywhere you wanna go, just as long as we're far away from here. Ever since I've been on this earth, New York has been nothing but pain. I mean, I miss my sisters and even my mom, but I have to make peace with the fact that I may never see them again." She started to shake at the mentioning of them. I could tell she was seriously emotionally affected by the subject of her peoples. That made me feel some type of way.

"Look, Jade, maybe you'll see your sisters again one day. Don't write it out of your mind just yet. For now, we have to do what is smart, and secure us so we can live to fight another day. Let's get this money. I think I know what to do with them bricks, too. I still got a few tricks up my sleeve."

She nodded. "Yeah, I bet you do." She hugged me tighter, then released me. "You cool?"

"Yeah."

I placed my hand on the door knob, and twisted, pulled it inward and stepped into the short hallway that led to the bedroom. When I got there, I scanned it for Santana and saw no trace of him. Not only was he gone, but so was the money and bricks I'd left on the bed. I ran to the small hotel closet and threw the door open, it was empty. Got on my knees and looked under the bed. Empty. I could feel my heart pounding in my chest. My throat became tight. My palms were sweaty.

I stood back up, looking around for any signs Santana would be coming back and found none, just as my phone buzzed.

Jade walked into the room and peered over it with her eyes. She shook her head and sat on the edge of the bed, before placing her hands over her face and lowering them to her thighs.

I read the text from Santana. It said: I'ma get all of your paper, den fuck wit you. My jail stint wasn't on you. So, give me a week or so and I'ma have all seventy-five racks. I ain't fuckin' wit you until then. That bitch changing you. Get ya mind right. One week, nigga.

I took the phone and threw it as hard as I could into the wall, breaking it into a hundred or more pieces, stood up with my heart pounding. That bitch-ass nigga had fucked me again. I was so mad my eyes were watering. We were back to the eight dollars, to square one. I couldn't believe that my right-hand man had screwed me again, expected me to wait around on him until he came up with the rest of the paper that was owed to me. That was dirty.

Jade removed her hands from her face and looked up to me. "He took all of the money?"

I nodded and stood there feeling defeated. "Yeah, he did. Say he gon fuck wit me in a week when he get the rest of it." I was so angry, I felt like punching somethin'.

Jade covered her face again and shook her head. "How long is this room paid up for?"

I shrugged my shoulders. "I think just until tomorrow afternoon. Check-out is always noon. That's universal for most hotels."

She smiled weakly. "Then, at least we should be thankful that we got some heat for the night. I say we chill and try to regroup. Getting mad, ain't gon do nothin' but make matters worse for the both of us. We have to have clear heads in order to master our struggles right now." She scooted over close to me and laid her head on my shoulder. "Don't worry, Bentley, we'll be okay. We're too strong not to be."

I wrapped my arm around her body and held her close. "I wish I could have that same faith you have, Jade. It's so hard though. I'm so mad right now that I don't know what to do. I feel like killing Santana."

There was a long pause, before she sat up and hugged me. "Come on, baby. How about you hold me for a little while? We'll get some rest. Enjoy this warmth and think about how we're going to survive in the winter storm out there. Come on." She kicked off her shoes and scooted backward on the bed. Peeled the comforter back and climbed under it, holding it open for me. "Come on, Bentley."

I sat there with my nostrils flared, seething. Santana would get his. I didn't know how I was going to make him pay for the shit he was taking us through, but when it was all said and done, I was gon make sure he paid for every minute of it.

"You comin?" she asked again.

I kicked off my Timbs and scooted up to her. I got under the covers and snuggled up behind her. "Us, Jade?"

"It's us," she whispered.

Chapter 7

Jade

I snuggled into the bus shelter beside Bentley as the wind blew harshly, while the snow fell in big blankets from the sky. It was already four inches of it in the ground, and the weatherman said there was more to come. He was calling it the Nor'easter and it was kicking our butts. It was freezing out. The wind howled as it traveled about, sending snowflakes about the air like little weapons. I'd been hit in the eye by more than a few. Tears seeped out of my eyes, and ran son my cheeks, before they were frozen. My toes and fingers were numb. I was shaking, and the bus shelter gave us very little protection from the storm because the windows had been busted out of it, as were majority of the bus shelters in New York.

Bentley pulled me closer to him and wrapped his arms around me. "Jade, look across the street. You see that white dude smoking that cigarette over there behind the dentist office?"

I glanced over and allowed my eyes to adjust. The snow was falling so rapidly it was hard for me to see through the fray. But once my eyes grew accustomed to the conditions, I was able to see exactly what he was talking about. "Yeah, I see him. What about him?"

"Yo, I think he rolling that Subaru over there. If he is, I'm finna holler at him. We need them wheels," he said, shaking. I knew he had to be freezing because in addition to shaking, all the while he spoke to me, his teeth were chattering together. I felt sorry for him and me, for that matter.

"What makes you think that man gon just give you his truck? It's below zero out here. What he gon do, give us his transportation so he can walk?" I asked, confused. I knew most people in New York were assholes, especially when it came to cold weather. I didn't know what made the cold bring out the asshole in them, but it did.

"N'all, I'm finna take his shit and see if he got some bread on him. Hopefully, he got a few hunnit. That'd be a major plus for us right now, seeing as we ain't got one red cent to our name. I know you hungry, because I am. I'm starving like Marvin, Jade." His eyes remained trained across the street.

I followed them. The man was smoking some sort of cigarette and talking on his cell phone. He appeared to be hollering into it and waving his free hand with the cigarette tucked between his fingers. He flicked it and continued to talk in his phone. "How you gon do that?"

He scooted away from me and lifted his coat. "With one of these." I saw the handle of his guns. They were chrome. They looked huge, scaring me for a second. I wondered where he'd gotten them from. I didn't remember seeing them ever since he'd left the trap house back in Harlem, right before I had my altercation with the police officer. "Baby, are you gonna kill him for it?" I suddenly felt paranoid and glanced back over to the man who appeared to be going on a tirade over the phone. His black trench coat looked expensive. He was without a hat, wore only ear muffs. He had a head full of snow and sandy red hair.

"Let's hope it don't come down to that. But, one thing is for sure, I'm finna get you up out of this cold. Stay here." He pulled down his jacket and took off across the street, allowed a car to roll past before he finished on his way.

The man replaced his phone in one of his pockets and seemed to be on his way to his truck. He trounced through the snow, with his head lowered, walking speedily. He got to the driver's side door, chirped the alarm and pulled open the door, just as Bentley ran up on him and grabbed him by the neck, pulled his chrome weapon and slammed it to the man's forehead.

"Shit," I muttered and ran across the street. I looked down the road and saw the city bus coming in our direction. When I got to the other side of the street, I ran beside Bentley, out of breath. "Baby, the city metro bus is coming. It should be packed, it's four o'clock, rush hour."

Bentley tightened his hold around the man's neck and squeezed. I could hear him gagging. He mugged me. His eyes seemed different. Colder. "I told you to stay ya ass over there. You ain't got shit to do wit this," he growled.

"I'm sorry, baby. But the metro bus is coming. I was starting to panic. I didn't know what to do, but I knew a metro bus full of people could spell a lot of trouble for us with all of the witnesses and whatnot."

There was a vicious scowl on his face. He attempted to look down the busy street in the direction of where the bus would be coming from. "It's good, baby. Don't trip, get in the truck."

"The truck?" I asked, stupidly. The adrenalin of the situation was messing with my common sense.

"Yeah, get in the truck. In the back."

I pulled open the door and got inside like he'd ordered me to. The truck was already warm because of the remote starter the man had used. There was a brief case on the seat of the door that I opened. I tossed it to the floor and sat down, rubbernecking to see what Bentley had up his sleeve next.

Bentley tossed the man into the truck and kept his pistol aimed at him. The man wound up on the center console. "What do you want me from me? If it's the truck, just take it. I swear, I won't call the cops until you're long gone."

Bentley yanked him up, slid across his body to the passenger's side of the truck. "You think I'm stupid. I know this truck got a tracking device in it that your company can pull up at any time. All of the new Subaru's do and this one is a 2019, the freshest one of them all. I ain't stupid. N'all, first thing you gon do is close that door. Then, you're going to slowly pull out of this lot, and we'll go from there. Go." He pushed him toward the driver's door but kept ahold of his jacket.

The man grabbed the handle to the door and slammed it closed, just as the city's metro bus came to a halt across the street. He put the truck in reverse and backed out of the parking space, then put it into drive and stopped before he pulled out of the lot. "Am I going east or west?" He dared to look over at Bentley. Then, his eyes grew wide. "Wait, I saw you on the news. You're that cop killer." He looked over his shoulder back to me. "And you're that girl. Holy fuck. Please don't kill me. I have close to a thousand dollars in my wallet. We can go to as many ATMs as you want. I won't put up a fight. I swear it." His face was beet red.

Bentley looked back at me. "Damn, babe." He shook his head and stuck the gun more forcefully into the man's neck. "Go east. Get on the highway, I'll tell you where to go from there."

The man nodded. "Just please don't kill me. I have two kids. And a wife. They need me. I'll do anything you want," he cried, making a left and stepping on the gas.

As he drove, Bentley was in and out of his pockets so fast it looked as if he were a professional. He tossed the wallet back to me. "Baby, see how much loot he got on him. He said it's almost a gee. It better be."

I opened the wallet and pulled out all of the bills before counting them. The total came to nine hundred and eighty-five dollars. "It's nine eighty-five," I reported.

"Yeah, and I have another forty-six grand in the bank. You can have every penny. Just don't kill me. Please."

"Shut up! Look, man, don't say that shit no more or I'ma do the opposite. That's getting real fucking annoying," Bentley snapped, poking him in the neck with the barrel. The man's head was bent at an awkward angle. "Take off that watch. And gimme that ring on your finger. Hurry up."

The man began to drive with one hand as he followed Bentley's orders, before handing him everything. "Are we stopping at an ATM?" he asked with his eyes on the road.

"Pull on to the interstate. Go," Bentley directed.

He was forced to stop at the red light that came directly before we were able to enter on to the highway. I looked ahead and saw how slow the traffic was moving on it. It would have taken us forever to get wherever we were going. "Baby, it's rush hour, remember? The interstate is jam packed and will be for the next two hours. We need to take an alternate route."

Bentley cursed. "Fuck, you're right. Damn." He turned back to hand me the jewelry. Handed me the watch and dropped the ring on the floor. As soon as the ring hit the floor, the white man used the diversion to open the driver's side door and then he jumped out of the truck.

He fell to the ground hard, then came to his feet and took off running. "Help! Help! Help!" He ran into the middle of oncoming traffic, causing cars to slam on their brakes to avoid hitting him.

One silver Toyota 4Runner tried to swerve to avoid him and wound up in the wrong lane, where it collided head-on with a minivan. The crunching of metal was loud enough to make me cringe. Then a red car crashed into the back of the 4Runner, and another car crashed into the back of that one. Some dude on a Harley Davidson swiveled to avoid the melee and succeeded only to swipe the man that had jumped out of the truck. He flew into the air and came down hard on his side, lying motionless.

Bentley jumped into the driver's seat and backed the truck away from the stop lights, made a backwards U-turn and brought the truck straight, before storming back into the direction we'd come from. He stepped on the gas. "Get up here, Jade, and put your seat belt on. We gotta get as far away from this area as possible."

The sirens resonated in the distance. I unhooked my seat belt, and almost slipped on the man's briefcase rushing to get into the front of the truck. Once there, I followed Bentley's commands. "Baby, where are we going?" I asked, looking over my shoulder to see how bad the scene behind had gotten. One of the cars was on fire.

"We gotta get out of New York. It's too hot here. We finna go fuck wit one of my high school buddies that live out in Camden, New Jersey. I ain't seen him in a while, but we were always tight. Camden a be a new scene for us. New York burnt the fuck up. We're on fire here." He made a left onto a residential street after seeing two police cars speeding in our direction. "Fuck, we gotta get out of here."

"Jersey is cool. Anything is better than New York. Seriously. I hate it here. The only good thing about it is that I met you here. Other than that, it's a cursed place to be."

He tried to make a right and the truck slid through the snow for approximately seven feet, and hopped the curb of the block, just before it stopped. My heart was pounding in my chest. The snow was coming down twice as hard. "Jade, you good?" he asked, looking over at me.

I nodded. "Yeah. Come on, take your time. Let's get out of here."

***

We slipped into a motel outside of Camden County, four hours later. It had taken us that long to get there because of how bad the roads were. Luckily, when we got to it, the place was being run by an old woman who looked to be in her nineties. We paid her a hundred dollars for two nights, and she handed over the keys without so much as a second glance in our direction.

Bentley came into the room and fell backward in the bed, exhaling loudly. "Damn, baby. I swear, if we ain't have no bad luck, then we wouldn't have any luck at all. Did you see what happened to that white dude? Fuck. Now watch they try and blame that shit on us. Fuck."

I climbed on the bed beside him and ran my hand across his chest, even though it was covered by his bomber jacket. "At least we got a lil money now. And this room? I mean, it's not much, but it is out of New York. We gotta be thankful for that."

He looked over at me and smiled. Then, he pulled me on top of him. "You're always so positive. I wish I could be more like that, but if shit don't go my way, then I see the worst in each situation. How do you stay so positive?" He rubbed my cheek.

I stared down at him, his scent invading my nose and causing me to feel some type of way. "Because no matter what, we still have each other. As long as we have us, I feel like we'll be able to overcome anything. Now give me them lips." I sucked his into my mouth and moaned. Somehow, we wound up on our sides, tonguing each other down. I unzipped his coat and pulled it off. He did the same to me. Then, I was on top of him. His hands roamed all over my breasts, squeezing them. They snuck under my shirt and were now on hot skin. I tossed my head back and moaned. "I'm ready, Bentley. I don't wanna think about nothing else. I'm ready. I'm ready right now."

He picked me up and tossed me back on the bed, pulled my shirt and then my bra off. Next came the jeans, and then my panties. Off my ankles they went and to the floor. He straddled my body. "I want you so bad, Jade. I swear to God, I'm feening for you. I been feening for you since day one, but I ain't gon do nothing unless you're really, really ready." He sucked my neck, and proceeded to lick all over it, massaging my breasts.

"I'm ready, Bentley. I want you. I want you so, so bad. Please." I spread my legs.

He slipped down my body and pushed my knees to my chest. He put his face in between my legs and sucked my lips into his mouth, licked all over them, before releasing them and opening the folds wide. I felt his tongue trailing circles around my clit, then he sucked on it. The noises were incredible, along with the feeling.

I shivered. "Un. Bentley. It feel so good, baby. It feels so, so good." I closed my eyes tight and bucked into his mouth. My essence poured out of me. So much so, I felt a puddle under my backside. Bentley squeezed my lips together, sucked on them like that, then attacked my jewel, flickering it over and over. "Uh! Uh! Baby! Baby! Aw, shit! Baby!" I screamed, embarrassed at myself.

What must Bentley think of me, I wondered for a split second, before my body began shaking so bad that I couldn't even focus any longer. Instead of him stopping, he kept at me, licking and slurping away at my juices. I tried to get away from him. My clit became too sensitive. But, he grabbed my ankle and went right back at me.

"This my pussy, Jade. Mine. You my baby. This is us!" Then his face was between my legs, moving from side to side, growling and sending me on a journey I couldn't hang with. I sat all the way up while he did his thing, screaming because of how amazing it felt. I fell backward on the bed shaking as if I were freezing, my lower abs still vibrating. More of my cream poured out of me, and into his mouth.

He licked up and down between my folds, sucking on my thighs. "I love this body, baby. You're so perfect to me. So fine, Jade. I gotta have some of you, boo. I can't take it no more." He stripped with lightning speed and got between my legs. He took the head of his penis and rubbed it up and down in between the gates of my garden. My cream continued to leak out of me. I felt his piece entering my channel, stretching me.

"Uh. Bentley. Be gentle." I dug my nails into his back, as he slammed his hips forward and broke through my barrier, implanting himself deep within my womb. I squeezed my eyes tight as tears spilled out of them. The stinging pain was mind numbing at first. I wanted to push him off of me.

He pulled back just a tad, then pushed forward again, then pulled all the way back, only to slam home hard. The feeling kept on getting better and better, until I was able to wrap my legs around his thrusting body.

"Un. Un. Un. Yes. Ooo. Bentley. Baby. Uhhh! Baby." I moaned as the bed squeaked under us. The headboard made a steady *tap, tap, tap* against the wall.

He grunted and sucked on my neck. "You're so perfect. Uh. You're so perfect, baby. Fuck, this so good. Huh. Huh. Aw, baby. Mmm." He picked up my thighs as he long stroked me. I could hear the audio of our sexes.

"Bentley. Baby. Un. Bentley. Bentley. It's happening again! Uh, baby! Shit?" My entire womb seemed to lock up and then a split second later, vibrate so hard that it felt like there was nothing down there but a party of pleasure.

Bentley sucked on my neck. "I'm cumming, Jade. I'm cumming, baby." His middle crashed into mine harder and harder, bringing about a sensual dose of pleasure and pain, before he fell on top of me, kissing all over my lips. "You're so perfect. So, so perfect, Jade."

I didn't know how I was going to feel the next morning because of this night. But, one thing is for sure. I felt physically amazing and had no regrets.

Chapter 8

Bentley

My mans, Guns, answered the door to his apartment with a big smile on his face, and had a blunt hanging from his lips that looked like a brown marker, it was so fat. When he saw me he took two steps back, and laughed. "Aw, hell n'all. Look at Mr. Fugitive. Cop killer. Daddy popper. Jack of all trades, Bentley. What it do, kid?" He stepped forward and wrapped me into his embrace.

Guns was five feet, six inches tall and real heavyset. He was dark as hell, with long dreads and dark brown eyes. We'd gone to Malcolm Shabazz High School together. He'd attended for the tenth and eleventh grade, then got locked up. He caught a shooting case in Trenton, and had been waived to the adult system. Throughout his bid, we'd stayed in contact and prior to that, he, Santana and I had a thing for stealing and jacking cars. We were obsessed with the movie *New Jersey Drive*, and tried to emulate the movie in real life. Guns had always been one hunnit percent a hussler. A go-getter. A street nigga like myself.

I stepped out of his embrace. "Yo, keep that nonsense on the low. The kid is innocent, Dunn. Me and my rib."

"Yo rib? Who is your rib, son?" He stuck his neck past me to look into the hallway. Looked both ways.

"Nigga, don't worry about it. Let me step in and get the fuck out of this hallway. I already know how they get down out here in the Peter McGuire Gardens. Yo, I can't believe you still stay in this dump." I walked past him into the apartment. The first thing I saw was a light-skinned chick, with her back to us in the kitchen, cooking something on the stove. She wore a pair of booty shorts that were all in her ass. She was nude from the waist up.

Guns strolled inside and closed the door. "Yo, the Gardens is home for me, my nigga. I ain't never leaving this bitch. My blood, sweat and tears are here." He followed my gaze to the kitchen. "I see you peeping my li'l bitch. She just turned eighteen yesterday. I been tearing that ass up ever since then."

I scoffed. "Hardly, I ain't thinkin' about shorty. Look, I need some cash, bruh. I'm talkin' like fast and plentiful. You already know my situation. I got the Jakes on my ass, trying to pin a bogus murder rap on the god. I need enough cash to get me and my woman as far as away from the East Coast as possible. Ain't shit here for me no more."

Guns smacked his lips and handed me the blunt. "That's the second time you done mentioned this broad, kid. Who is she?"

I sat on the couch, taking tokes of the bud. "Don't worry about all of that. You got some gigs lined up or what?" It didn't take more than a few pulls and I was lifted. The loud had me floating. My eyelids turned into slits and I got to feeling real mellow.

The yellow chick came out of the kitchen with a baloney sandwich on a plate, cut down the middle. There were plain potato chips on the side of it and in the other hand, she held a grape soda. Her titties bounced on her chest as she leaned over to set the plate in front of Guns. "Here you go, daddy. I hope you like it." She kissed him on the cheeks and sat on the couch in the middle of us.

Guns looked over to me and smiled. "You see how thick my project shorty is. Huh?"

"What?" I asked, looking at this nigga like he'd lost his mind. The last thing on my mental was the shape of his woman. I needed money and I needed it immediately.

70

"Stand up, baby. Show my nigga all that ass. Let me explain to him why I ain't left the projects."

She stood up and turned around in front of us. The shorts were all in her booty. She had to be at least thirty-eight inches from the waist down. Her top was just as voluptuous. "Is he looking, daddy?" She popped back on her legs and spread them, and this made the shorts disappear even further into her backside.

"Yeah, he looking. That's good, baby. Gon into the back room until daddy come and get you."

She licked her juicy lips and left the living room. "Don't be too long, daddy. I need you. I need some more birthday spanks." She disappeared down the short hallway and closed the bedroom door. I could hear the sounds of the springs as she sat on the bed on the other side of the door.

"That's why I ain't leaving, my nigga. It's one of them that turn eighteen in this mafucka every week." He busted up laughing.

I didn't join him. My mind was on getting right so I could move me and Jade up off of the East Coast. We needed to flee and fast. "That's what up, bruh. I'm happy you're enjoying yourself here. Now back to the money. What's good?"

He took the blunt back and took three hard pulls from it. I got some shit lined up. Jack moves, but it's rough and rugged though. The capers I'm talking about might get a nigga killed. You feel me?"

I leaned in with interest. "Where, when, how many capers, and how much you talking about per caper?" The palm of my right hand began to itch. That was always a sign of money to come for me.

The licks vary. One here. One in D.C., and one in Brooklyn. All three should be a minimum of twenty gees a piece, plus product. The one in Brooklyn should be double that."

I wasn't fuckin wit the one in Brooklyn. That woulda been going backward. That wasn't something I was willing to do, it didn't matter how much money was involved. But, I had to keep him on the hook, and not let him know the thoughts going through my mind. As long as I painted the picture of myself rolling with him no matter what, Guns was more susceptible to leading me down the yellow brick road of kick doors. "That sound good. So, which one you tryna hit first?"

"This one trap in D.C., they move that tar baby out of that bitch. One of the lil homies from right here in Camden pop out of there. He say it's sweet. For the blueprints, all he want is a few bricks so he can do his thing back home. I saved his ass a few months ago. Some Mexicans out in Newark were trying to knock his head off for some gambling debts. But, before they could, I took a good look at 'em. You know, let 'em see what that Kay sound like when that bitch screaming." He laughed and dumped the ashes from the blunt into the ashtray. "In exchange, he putting me up on this lick, and gave me the green light to fuck wit that yella ho in the room back there. You know how it go, one hand washes the other."

"Fa sho. How can I be down? I want it."

"If I cut you in, then that means I gotta cut that twenty in half. That leave me wit ten. I can't wipe my ass wit that. Now, if you was willing to take five and maybe a brick of the product, then maybe we could work something out. Unless, you into that hit shit. If you are, you could make ten gees a body, fifteen depending on who they are." He smoked the blunt down until it was a little bitty duck, then he left it in the ashtray.

"Nigga, it's whatever. I'm down for the cause as long as I can get my chips up front. I'll even take that five gees a trap you was talking about. I don't need the work. Just make that shit happen."

He picked up the baloney sandwich and bit it with his eyes closed. "Yo, you got a phone?"

"N'all, I had to ditch my old one. I need one too, why you got one for me?"

He nodded. "Yeah, I just got a shit load of these iPhone X joints. My li'l bitch work for Verizon, so I'ma hook you up before you leave with the works. Long as you fuckin' wit me, don't worry about the bill. I gotchu."

"That's what's up. I'ma need two of them bitches though."

He laughed. "Of course, you are."

***

Two nights later, we were parked in his Suburban, sitting on a dark residential street, in the middle of another snowstorm. It was so cold outside that the windshield wipers were frozen. It had taken us fifteen minutes to even get his truck started. We were at our first lick that was to take place in Washington Heights, which was the Spanish section of Camden.

"Kid, why are we over here on the Latino side of town? What's good?"

He slid black leather gloves on to his hands, then reached under his seat and came up with an automatic .44 Desert Eagle, with an extended clip. I had one of my Glocks on me. I felt secure, and ready to make my first piece of change.

"The other night when you was over at the apartment, I could tell you were in need of some serious cash, so I figured, why not go hard right out the gate? We can get ten bands apiece, and whatever else is in the house. The only thing is that we gotta smoke this Screech cat. The fellas put that paper on his head and I wanna cash in on it. He stay wit his baby mother in that spot right across the way. Some bum bitch. She on that raw real heavy. He is too."

I glanced across the street at the duplex. The walkway looked like it needed to be shoveled. The snow was piled so high that it was a mystery as to how they got in and out of their crib. "So, we wetting this nigga for the twenty?"

He nodded. "That's the plan. You got a problem wit that?" He laid a black ski mask on my lap.

"Hell, n'all." I slid it over my face, and cocked my Glock. "Let's get it. Wait, how we gon get in this mafucka to handle our bidness?" I reached for the door handle, then stopped.

Guns made sure his ski mask was straight, then gazed over to me. "We gon kick that bitch in. That's what I'm accustomed to. I know how to wreck the doors. Knock the locks off of the hinges wit one kick. Let's mob out."

I stopped him. "Wait a minute. Yo, you know how the dope heads be ringing doorbells, asking if they can shovel your snow and shit all winter? Just to see if they can come up on a few bucks?"

He nodded. "Yeah, what about it? You tryna shovel snow for some scratch and shit? Hell, n'all. That's bum shit."

"N'all, but you see how much snow in front of their crib? It's all on the porch and everything."

"And?"

"And, that's how we get them to open the door. We act like we wanna shovel the snow, then when that door open up, we handle bidness. It's as simple as that."

"Yo, that's what's good. Hell, yeah. Come on." He opened the door to his Suburban and jumped out of it, with me in tow.

The block was real dark. I couldn't spot any street lights and for us, that was a good thing. It meant we could work under the cover of darkness. Guns jogged a bit, holding his hand under his puffy Sean John coat. When he got to the mark's

74

house, he had to take huge steps to track through the snow. There was a Cadillac Escalade parked in front of the residence, and foot prints leading from the truck all the way up to the house. There was only a bit of snow covering them, so I knew they were nearly fresh. I laid my hand on the hood of the truck to feel how warm it was. I felt the heat and knew it had been turned off recently. I slipped my glove back onto my hand and jogged across the yard, taking big steps like Guns. By the time I got on to the porch, my calves, along with my toes were frozen. Guns nodded his head at me and stepped to the side of the door.

I moved to the right side of the door and rang the doorbell that was lit up. There was a small rectangular window in the upper center of the door that had a mini curtain over it. I worried that the sight of us with masks on would prevent them from opening the door. I didn't like the conventional way of how most niggas pulled kick doors. There had been a lot of the homies back in Brooklyn that had lost their lives, attempting to kick somebody's door in. I didn't know this stud Screech from Adam. Not his habits, his ways. His thought process, nothing. So in my book, he could have been holding anything on the other side of the door. The risk of trying to kick his shit in and us getting hit up was a fear of mine. This was still New Jersey, New York's cousin.

A female with dark circles around her eyes pulled the curtain back and tossed her long, yet frazzled hair over her shoulder. She scratched her scalp. "Yeah, what do you want?" she asked, looking out at me, with eyes wide open.

"Your snow, ma'am. Can I shovel your snow to make a quick five dollars? Please. I'm tryna feed my kid."

She looked past my shoulder out to the conditions of the porch, and the front yard. Then somebody must have called her because she turned around and got to hollering something to somebody inside of the house, before turning back to me. "Yeah, that's cool. Hey, but get the back pathway too. I'll give you five for the front, and five for the back. Let me know when you're done." She left from the window and fixed the curtain back.

I stood there frozen in place. Looked around the yard and got ready to lose my mind. There was no possible way I was going to shovel their fuckin' snow, just to hit this lick. That could have taken us all night, then there was no telling what could have taken place in that amount of time.

Guns stepped over to me. "Now what? Yo, I ain't shoveling no fuckin' snow, B. I'm about to kick this bitch off of the hinges and call it a day. I ain't got no time for that and all this other shit. Step back, let me handle this shit." He stood in front of the door, took two steps back, as I stepped to the side of him. Then, I heard the locks popping on the door, and it began to open. I rushed to the side of it. Guns stood there in the ready.

The same female from earlier, opened the door all the way with a light spring jacket draped around her shoulders. "Huh, I'ma trust you and give you your money up front. Here you go." She handed the ten-dollar bill out to Guns, and instead of him taking it, he grabbed her arm, and slammed the butt of his gun into her forehead so hard that it dropped her. She fell to the porch and I stepped over her and ran into the house. The first thing I smelled was a heavy stench of crack. The entire house had a thick cloud of crack smoke looming in the air, so much so that it had me coughing. My throat burned. When I got to the living room, there was a Mexican dude sitting on the couch with a brick of yay open on the table, and beside that one was two more. He was smoking the pipe and was without a shirt. There were tattoos all over him, including his face. He was puffing away as if his life depended on it. When he saw us rush into the room, he dropped the pipe and hopped over the couch, making a dash for the back of the house.

"That's Screech, B! Hit his ass!" Guns yelled, aiming.

I upped my gun and aimed.

Boom. Boom. Boom.

He flew into the hallway's wall and fell. "Ay! Mutha-fucka!"

Guns ran up on him and let loose. "Cha-ching, mutha-fucka."

Boom. Boom. Boom.

His bullets rocked Screech, leaving a bloody mess. "Grab those bricks off of the table and let's go!" he ordered.

I did just that before we rushed out of the crib and jumped over Screech's bitch. Guns stopped short and got ready to finish her off, but I stopped him. "N'all, bruh, she ain't on shit. The hit was for that nigga. Let's go."

He stood there for a moment with his gun aimed down at her, then kicked her as hard as he could in the stomach. She rolled on her back and groaned, still knocked out from the blow he'd given her to the head. "She lucky, Dunn. Lucky. Come on."

Chapter 9

Jade

Bentley stepped into the motel room and dropped a bundle of cash on the bed, along with his pistol. I was standing by the dresser rubbing lotion into my hands. He came over to me and pulled me into his arms, holding me tight. The cold from his jacket made me shiver. He kissed my neck. "I missed you, baby. I been thinking about you all day long. I mean, all day." That made me smile. "I been thinking about you too, Bentley. Worried out of my mind. Where have you been?"

He hugged me and released me. He went into his coat pocket and handed me a cell phone. "Here, it's already activated, and don't worry about the bill. I got that. This money should last us for a few days. There's more what that came from, and I paid up our motel bill until the end of the month, though I'm hoping to have us with enough bread to be long gone before then." He pulled out another phone and set it on the dresser, unzipped his big coat and hung it in the closet. He exhaled and sat on the edge of the bed.

I came and stood in front of him and ran my hand over the top of his waves. "Baby, you still haven't answered my question. Where have you been all night? It's five in the morning. You left out of here at two 'o'clock yesterday."

"Baby, that's ten gees on the bed. We can get us right wit that. We got phones now. Unlimited data and all the extras. We're good. It shouldn't matter where I was, just as long as I'm making it happen for us. You feel me?"

I stepped back and placed my hand on my hip. "Excuse me? So, you think that just because you went out there and bussed a few moves that it's okay for you to come in when you feel like it? To have me worrying about you, not knowing if I'll ever see you again? You think that money is worth all of that? Well, it ain't. It just ain't, Bentley. Now, where were you? I want specifics. This is us." I grabbed his face and made him look up at me. My anger was building, along with my possession over him.

He exhaled again. "Damn, baby. I don't want you knowing about the shit I do in those streets. I wanna keep you as far away from that lifestyle as I can. You're so pure, Jade. I gotta keep you that way. You ain't all corrupted like me and shit. I been fucked in the game ever since my beginning. But you, you're different." He stood up, and walked away from me, into the bathroom and grabbed a face towel, ran the water in the sink, before washing his face.

I pursued him. "This is us, Bentley. Where were you? What did you have to do for that money? Don't shield me like I can't handle the truth. Don't treat me like I'm less than you are, because we're in this shit together. You and I are one now. So, talk to me." I turned him around. "What did you do?"

"I smoked a nigga, alright?" He stepped past me, back into the main room of the small motel. "That's what I'ma have to do to get our bands up. I'ma have to smoke a few niggas and run in a few traps. Once we get about fifty gees, we should be able to move off of the East Coast. To where, I don't know? I haven't thought that far. My main concern is getting the money first." He pulled his shirt off. Took his pistol and placed it under the pillow of his side of the bed. Then, he took his pants off.

I didn't know what to say or do. Murder was serious. I was being charged with one that I was innocent of, and it was damning to my soul. So, I could only imagine what really went on inside of him. I knew he was only doing it for the betterment of us, and that made me feel some type of way as well. I hated for him to feel as if he had to do it all alone. I wish there was some way I could assist him. I hated feeling so dependent and more of a burden than his woman. But, even though I was from the Red Hook Houses, I wasn't from the streets. My parents had kept me so sheltered that all of this was new to me. I was familiar with waking up, going to school, after school programs, and then back home. Church was on Wednesdays and Sundays. Other than that, I was staring out of my project window, unable to leave the confines of my parent's place.

"I gotta get us right, Jade. I don't care who I gotta smoke, or what I gotta do. All that matters to me is us, you and I. Come here and let me hold you for a minute. I need you."

I turned around to face him and smiled weakly, then climbed in the bed, and into his arms. He felt and smelled so good. He held me firmly, kissed my forehead. "Bentley, how does what you're doing for us make you feel? Honestly, too. I don't want none of those cliché, tough guy's responses. I want the truth."

He kissed my cheek. "It's the only way, baby. I gotta play the hand that we were dealt. I am not the dealer. I gotta do whatever it takes. I been in these streets for as long as I can remember, Jade, bussing moves and doing wrong, and this is the first time that I'm doing it for a cause that means something to me. I'm crazy about you. So, if I gotta get knee deep in blood until we get to where we need to be, then so be it. I feel nothing."

I rested my cheek against his. "Baby, I don't like you putting your life on the line for us. I understand what you're trying to do, and why you're doing it, but I can't lose you. You cannot be the only one out here trying to make it happen for us. I have to do something, and if I don't then what am I good for then?"

He brought his hands around and held my waist, then pulled me on top of him. He trailed his hands down to my backside, gripping my ass. "Baby, all I need is for you to be here when I get back each time. That's it. I'll roam those jungles out there and bring back what we need. I'll stare death in the eyes and make it bow down. As long as I got you, and you're here all about me, that's enough." He pulled me down and kissed my lips, sucking on the bottom one and running his tongue across it, before kissing me hard. "You're my baby, Jade. As long as I'm able to make it happen, you ain't gotta do shit. I mean that.

His kisses trailed down to my neck. He added teeth, then sucked hard, breathing heavy. Mine became labored as well. My nipples spiked. I felt a weird tingling in my stomach. "I wanna do more, Bentley. I wanna be out there with you. I don't like this helpless feeling. I am a queen, not a dependent. Un, baby. You gotta let me do more."

He flipped me over and kissed all over my breasts through my shirt. Pulled on my nipples with his teeth, before removing the shirt altogether. "N'all, ma. That's what I'm here for. I got this. Never consider yourself a dependent. We are equals. Everything you do for me is the reason I do what I do for you. You're my baby. It ain't for you to be out in those streets. That's a man's job." He palmed my breasts, pushed them together, and sucked on both of the nipples hard, alternating. "Damn, these titties are so pretty. That's the first thing I noticed when I saw them. I told myself that they were the prettiest I've ever seen in my life, as is all of you. I ain't never been obsessed with a female before, but now I am. I'm crazy about you, Jade." He sucked my nipples and worked down my body, licking and sucking until his tongue hit my boy shorts. He licked up and down the crotch, and in between the space where my thigh and pelvic bone met.

I bucked on the bed. "I wanna do more, Bentley. I wanna ride for you like you do for me. You're my baby, too. I'm just as obsessed with you."

My panties were pulled off of my ankles, then his face entered the apex of my thighs, before he started to send me on a journey with his lips and tongue. I mean, he catered to every portion of my body down below, smacking and slobbering all over them. When his lips trapped and began to suck on my jewel, I thought I might go crazy, and lose my mind.

"Uhhhhh! Bentley! Bentley. Why won't you listen to me?" I screamed, cumming hard on his assaulting tongue.

His fingers entered my channel, they moved at full speed in and out of me. "This my pussy, Jade. Mine. This all I need. You're all I need." He flipped me on my side and got behind me. Took his piece and slowly entered my garden and got to hitting it hard from the side while he sucked on my neck. "You belong to me. You're my baby. I ride for you. Uh. Fuck, Jade. I ride for you. Gimme this pussy, ma. Forever." He took ahold of my hips and used them to make me slam back into him at full speed. I could feel his dick hitting my bottom before it came all the way out, only to slide back into me again. His big hand cupped my right breast. The hard nipple poked through the crack of his fingers. "Uh. Fuck. It's. So. Good."

I closed my eyes. Reached behind me and took ahold of his butt and urged him to go deeper. Harder. Faster. The feeling was so amazing. With every stroke, sparks flew through me, brought me closer to my climax. "Un. Bentley. You're so deep, baby. So damn deep," I moaned.

He sped up and turned me over onto my stomach. He climbed on top of me, slid back in and took of hold of my shoulders, hammering me. From this position I could feel him in my stomach. "Bentley. Baby. Oh. Baby. Please. Aw, shit baby. You're. Aw, my God!"

He bit into the back of my neck, slamming into me, before cumming repeatedly, jerking like crazy.

Chapter 10

Bentley

"Come on, baby, in order for you to ride beside me like you saying, you gotta at least be able to smoke this dog. He fucked up anyway. That other pit shook him too long, he on his way out," I said, stepping back.

Jade stood with the .380 in her hand, shaking like a leaf. She looked so cute all bundled up in her big puffy coat, with the scarf wrapped around her face. She wore a pair of gold Timbs that for some reason, made her look so sexy to me. We were on the roof of the Peter McGuire Housing Projects. I'd tied a red nose pit bull up by its hind legs, after Guns had used it to fight another pit bull that had shook him nearly to death. I figured since the dog was on its way out and needed to be put down, what better way to teach Jade how to shoot a pistol, and about death? So after the dog fight had been moved from the roof to one the empty apartments of the projects, me and Jade stayed behind, and now was the time for her lesson.

The snow flurried from the sky. The sun peeked through the clouds but did very little to warm me. It had to be less than ten degrees out. The roof was covered with thick fluffy snow.

Jade looked over to me as the dog coughed and began to bark. Smoke from the cold rose from its mouth. "Babe, I don't think I can do this. It's a dog. I wouldn't feel right killing it. Besides, when the gun pops, it sounds so loud. It makes my ears ring. Is there a way I can plug them first?"

I was trying my best not to get frustrated with her. I was already extremely reluctant about putting a gun in her hand to begin with. But, with the life we lived, I knew it was imperative for her to learn how to pop that cannon. So, I took a deep breath, and stepped behind her, kissed the small portion of her exposed cheek. "Yo, this mutt on his way out the game anyway. You gotta put him down, or else he gon suffer and wind up dying a long drawn out painful death. He's being tortured right now. Look at him."

She glanced over to him, stared and shook her head. "Aw-uh. Poor animal."

"Jade. Come on, stop that shit, ma. Now, you gotta be prepared for the unknown. There isn't time in those streets to be thinking about how whatever you're about to kill is feeling. Fuck that dog. Hate that dog. Smoke that dog. It's as simple as that. Now come on." I got behind her and held her tight made her lift the gun. "Aim at his bitch ass, and shoot. Fuck him."

She slid her finger over the trigger and sighed. "I don't know who you think you talking to, Bentley, but you need to watch your tone. This is my first time. Damn. Use some patience."

"I'm sorry, baby. That's my bad. But I need that killa shit to come out of you quick. Them people on the news are saying that we're armed and dangerous. Our reward is up to five hundred thousand, and we got every blue uniform in the state of New York looking for us. It's only a matter of time before it spills over to Jersey, so we gotta be prepared for the unknown. Now smoke that punk ass dog. Now. Just imagine that he bit ya man and tried to takes hold of my throat. Can you do that? Imagine he tried to kill me. Your Bentley, ma. What would you do?"

She sniffled, raised the gun, and pulled the trigger repeatedly.

Boom. Boom. Boom. Boom.
Click. Click. Click.

86

The first three bullets missed the dog altogether, but the last four put big holes into the animal's body. It yelped three times, before hanging with its tongue outside of its mouth.

"There. You proud of me?" she asked, lowering the gun, and attempting to look back at me. Smoke rose from the barrel.

I kissed her cheek. "Hell yeah, I am. That's a start. Now come on, we gon try and move you through the ranks of your training right away. The focal is to turn your heart as cold as possible. Very little can be done in these streets if your heart isn't cold. So, from here on out, the only thing I want you to care about besides yourself is me. Fuck the rest of the world and everything up in it. It's all about you and me. You got that?"

She nodded. "Wait, but I can't love my sisters no more?"

"Yeah boo, you can still love them, but have a distance, love. Push the feelings that you have for them into the back of your heart, like I had to do with my mother. The only person in this world right now that I love is you, Jade. Don't nobody else come close. So fuck 'em. Come on, let's get out of here." I got ready to jog toward the roof's door.

She grabbed my wrist. "Wait, baby."

I stopped and looked down at her. "What ma, we gotta get off of this roof before Housing Authority show up."

She moved her scarf backward and smiled. "I love you, too."

"Huh?"

She rolled her eyes. "You just said that you loved me, and I'm telling you that I love you too. You're the first man I have ever loved and will probably be the last."

Damn she had a way of bringing that soft shit out of me. I took the .380 out of her hand, and put it on my waist, fixed my shirt and coat, before snatching her to me. "Well, I do love you, Jade. I ain't never loved no female other than my mother. But, you're my baby. That's why I gotta go hard for you. Come on."

"Wait. Damn. Now that we done exchanged our I love you's, can a girl get a kiss or something?" She tilted her chin upward and closed her eyes.

I laughed. "No doubt." I sucked her lips into my mouth, before kissing her as if I was never going to see her again.

***

Guns slapped a fifty-round clip into his AR-33 assault rifle and cocked it back. He puffed on the blunt in the corner or his mouth and exhaled the smoke through his nose. "For this next li'l mission, the homies gon hit my hand with five bands, just to spray some down with this boy right here. Got some new niggas over in Collingswood that's trying to corner the market with that tar shit. They gotta be from Philly or somethin', I don't know. But, bruh 'nem want they trap to feel these slugs, so that's what we gon do. Huh, this twenty-five hunnit right here. Half."

I took the hunnits and counted them, made sure they added up to the amount he said. After confirming they did, I tucked the bills into my pocket. "So, you finna be on some drive-by shit. Ain't that kind of early nineties type shit?"

He shrugged his shoulders. "I don't know what era it's from, but we accepted their chips, so we gotta handle this bidness. It's as simple as that. If you ain't fuckin' around then just let me get that paper back and I'll go handle this tonight on my own."

"You got me fucked up. Ain't no refunds in this shit. I don't give a fuck who we hitting. Let's go so we can come on back. This ain't gon be my first time airing some shit out and won't be the last either. What's good with that other information I asked you about?"

He smiled. "I'm working on that as we speak. I got my li'l Rican bitch hollering at her peoples. As soon as she get back to me on them identifications, passports and all of that shit, I'ma let you know. I saw the latest news bulletin, kid. I know you're in much need, so I'ma make it happen. Oh yeah, before I forget. You know that nigga Santana hit me up last night, talking about he got that scratch for you, and he wanna hit yo hand when he get back from Detroit in three days. He say he been hitting yo phone, but that bitch saying it's no longer activated, so I texted him your new number this morning. He fucked wit you yet?" As he said this, the phone in his lap vibrated. He looked at the face and stood up.

I clenched my jaw over and over, heated at the mentioning of Santana's name. I felt bad blood for that nigga after how he'd done me. A part of me wanted to meet back up with him, just to blow him off of the map. "N'all, he ain't got at me. But, that's typical of him though."

Guns held up a finger. Held the phone to his ear. "So, you saying right now then? Denny's? Which one? Aiight. It's done. Have that later, I'll be to scoop it, believe that. One." He hung up the phone. "Bruh, we finna go sweat them niggas right now. They over at this Denny's on 32nd Street, in them Hilltop Boys' territory. Bruh say he got it to where his lil bitch situated them so they are sitting in front of the window. We gotta move right now." He bent down, and drug another AR-33 rifle from the bottom of the couch, then went back under it and grabbed a clip. Smacked it into the bottom of it, then stood up. "This one yours right here. This bitch got eighty shots. I want you to use every shot in it, whether you hit one of them niggas or not. Bruh just want them to know it ain't sweet."

I slid the gloves onto my hands and picked it up. "Let's bounce then, what the fuck are we waiting for?"

***

Forty-five minutes later, Guns brought the brown Ford Econoline van to a halt in front of the Denny's. He parked it and climbed over to the passenger's side, rolled down the windows just as I threw open the van's side doors, cocked the assault rifle, and aimed at the window where it looked to be about ten niggas sitting eating their food.

"That's them, bruh. That's them niggas." He set his rifle on the windowsill and squeezed the trigger.

Thaaat. Thaaat. Thaaat. Thaaat.

The window to the Denny's shattered and fell inward. I saw five of the dudes stand up, and immediately get filled with holes. Guns kept on spitting.

I squeezed my trigger and sprayed from right to left. Not trying to hit anybody in general, even took time to aim at the ceiling of the restaurant. Twenty-five hundred wasn't enough for me to have blood on my hands. This was supposed to be a scare tactic, so that's what I was treating it as, but not Guns. He was shooting to kill.

The assault rifle continued to jump in my hands, before it clicked empty. As soon as it did, I closed the side door and jumped into the driver's seat and pulled away from the curb. Stepped on the gas and sped down the snow-covered street, with the windshield wipers swishing from side to side. "Yo, you hit a few of them niggas up, Dunn. I thought you said you were just trying to scare they ass!" I hollered.

He laughed, rolling up the window. "N'all, bruh told me the price went from five to fifteen. Told me all I had to hit was one of them. But, you know how that rapid shit work. These bullets come out three at a time, and bullets ain't got no names on 'em, so it is what it is."

"Sound like you owe me at least five more gees, then," I said, a bit irritated. I didn't like going into missions blindly. If he knew what it was before we pulled up, then I should have known as well. But instead of getting into an argument with him about his negligent communication, I fell back and kept my comments to myself. "So, when we touch back down to your pad, I got that scratch coming, right?"

He nodded and scratched his beard. Sat the rifle under his seat and sat back. "Most definitely. I know you about your cheese, kid, and you need it more than me right now. I gotchu."

That was all I cared about. All the rest of those words ain't mean shit to me. I just needed to keep stacking my paper. That was the most important thing to me. I had to get me and Jade up off of the East Coast.

T.J. & Jelissa

Chapter 11

Jade

"Alright now, baby, you can come on out. I'm ready," Bentley yelled from the other side of the bathroom door.

I took a deep breath and opened it. I came out of the bathroom and stepped into a pitch dark room with scented candles burning all around it. They smelled like vanilla. He had them on top of the dresser, along the bed, the nightstand, and all over the floor. He was knelt in the center of the room with a bouquet of red roses in front of him, with his right hand behind his back. I looked around astonished. "Baby, what is all this?"

The candle lights shimmered off of his handsome face. "Come here, baby, and stand in front of me. I wanna tell you something."

"What's the matter, Bentley? You're acting kind of weird." It felt like I had a bunch of butterflies inside of my tummy. I felt nervous and all kinds of jittery. I stepped up to him. Took a deep breath and looked down.

This had been our official third week inside of the motel. It was December thirty-first, of two thousand eighteen. Eleven fifty-five at night, and he had our room covered with candles. To say that I was thrown off would have been an understatement.

He grabbed my hand. "Baby, I don't know what tomorrow holds, but all I know is that I love you with everything I am as a man. You're my heart. My soul. My baby, and my rib. And even though I know our days are numbered, I just wanna add that wife title to all the rest of them. With that being said, will you be my wife, my spouse, my forever?" He pulled a box from behind his back and popped it open. Inside was a diamond ring that sparkled even in the candlelight.

I started to shake. My knees got weak. I knelt beside him and couldn't take me eyes off of the ring. Peered back into his eyes, saying, "Baby, are you serious?"

He took the ring from the box and took a hold of my left hand. Held my fingers. "I love you, Jade. And I know we can't go in front of no judge and all of that, but we can say our vows in front of that God you believe in so much. I was doing some research online, and did you know that back in the old biblical times, they didn't have to go before no judge or nothing like that to make it official. The man and the woman made their vows before God and that was that. I know I ain't shown much interest in your Bible, but if it means that I can have you as my wife, I'll start. You mean the world to me. I need you as my wife. So, what do you say, baby? Will you marry me? Be my best half for the rest of my life?"

I was starting to shake, looking down at the ring, and then back up to his handsome face. I didn't understand why he wanted me so bad. Why he chose to trap so hard for me. Or how his love could be so unconditional, but thus far he hadn't shown me anything outside of that. Bentley was like a dream, a bad boy that all good girls yearned for. Not only was he written on the tablet of my heart, but he'd found a way to entwine himself with my soul. I love him to death.

"Baby, if you can promise me that your love will not change a week, a month, or even twenty years from now, then I would be honored to be your wife, and to have you as my husband." I wiggled the fingers on my left hand. "Yes, yes, yes. Put it on, baby. Put it on."

He laughed, kissed the back of my hand, then slid the ring on to my finger. He pulled me to him aggressively and kissed my lips with so much passion that I melted into his embrace. He fell backward after checking to make sure no candles were in our way. I straddled him and pulled his black beater over his head, kissing his juicy lips and smacking on them. "I love you, Bentley. You're my husband. I'ma ride for you, baby. Just watch." I licked a path along his neck, then traveled to his muscular chest. I ran my fingers over the scar tissue from the wound he sustained as a child, before lowering my lips to it. I licked it with my tongue, then sucked it. "I love you so much." He moaned as my tongue circled his nipples. "Mmm. I love you too, Jade. I'll die for you, baby. I'm your sacrifice. Just like your Bible say I'm supposed to be." He pulled my blouse over my head and unhooked my bra from the front, releasing my breasts.

I sucked down his rock hard abs, licked down the middle of the thick crack, and took time to caress and softly bite all eight individual muscles. I got down to his boxers and pulled them down his strong thighs. There was light hair on them. They felt firm. I took the boxers off of his ankles and kissed back up his legs. When I got to his penis and took ahold of it, sniffing the head. His scent always drove me crazy. It was Bentley's scent. The first man who truly loved little ole me. His penis swelled in my hand like a hot, thick light saber. I stroked it and kissed the side of it. "This belongs to me now Bentley. This is my piece. I ain't playin' about you from here on out. You got that? I vow before Jehovah to love and honor you for the rest of my life. Faithfully, and true. I promise my loyalty, devotion, and to kill for you, Bentley. All we have is us." His penis was so hard that it jumped in my hand. I could feel the thick veins of it.

"All we got is us, Jade. Damn, I love you, my rib." He leaned back and started to breathe heavy.

I licked my lips and slid his head into my mouth, sucking on it. I twirled my tongue around it over and over, then sucked him into my mouth as far as I could handle it. I gagged, and pulled him out. His taste was savory. This was my man. My protector. My rib bearer. My husband.

He shook. "Jade, handle me, baby. Please. Ma, you feel so good. Please handle me. You're my wife."

My head disappeared in his lap, sucking tight, and fast. My jaws hollowed in and out. My left hand stroked his long pole as I did my thing, slurping and making noises I knew would drive him crazy.

"Uh. Shit. Jade. My wife." He humped off of the floor, groaning, and whimpering deep within his throat. His head went from side to side.

My head was a blur. I wanted him to cum. I wanted to taste his seed. Wanted to know I could get him there, that I could make him cum hard all by myself. His pleasure would be my trophy. My fist pumped. My mouth sucked, harder and harder. Spit ran off of my chin and down his thick, long pole. I increased my speed.

"Uh. Uh. Jade. I'm finna cum, ma. I'm finna cum. Damn, boo. Damn." He laid all the way back and jerked on the floor, grunting and cumming into my mouth, coating it with his cream that was both salty and sweet. The essence of my man.

I stroked and swallowed, squeezed his pipe and brought the semen to the top of his penis, licking it off. I felt empowered having made my man cum, while making the noises that he made.

He picked me up and set me in the middle of the bed, flipped me onto my stomach, and pulled my panties down and off. He took one of the roses and tore the petals off and sprinkled them all over my backside, before licking all over both moons. He opened me up, and trailed his tongue up and down my crack, sucked on my sex lips, pulling on them, sendingg shivers through me.

"Mmm! Baby. Open me. Suck my jewel. Please, Bentley. I want you so bad." I came to my knees, shaking in anticipation of what he was going to do to me. I could feel my juices trickling down my inner thigh. I could still taste him on my tongue. I rolled it all around my mouth to savor it. This was my man.

Bentley attacked my kitten right away. He opened the lips wide, flicked his tongue across my clitoris over and over sending shocks through me, then he was sucking on it like a hard nipple while his big hand squeezed my ass, smacking it every few seconds. "You're mine, Jade." More licking, and sucking. "Mine. I'll kill a nigga over you. A bitch, too. They can't take us alive, Jade. We ain't going down without a fight. Not me and my rib." His face forced its way into my crease, and went to work.

I fell on my stomach and he kept on going. He had my pussy lips wide open, his tongue twirling all around the jewel, and flicking it harder and harder. I couldn't take it no more. "Bentley! Bentley! I'm cumming! I'm cumming! Oh my God!" I grabbed the sheets, careful to not pull them too much because of the candles. He continued to slurp, until he brought me to another earth shattering orgasm. Then he flipped me over and slid into my entrance, stabbed deep, pulled back and slammed it home again. "Give hubby this pussy, Jade. This mine now! All mine. You hear me?" He started to slide in and out of me at full speed, sinking deeper and deeper. My knees were pressed to my shoulder blades. I could feel my sex lips sucking at him. My essence oozed out of me and coated his shaft, gave him the lubrication he needed to hit the deepest regions of my womb at a rapid pace. His width was enough to drive me crazy. It took so much of my womanhood to accommodate his size.

He forced me into a ball and really turned into an animal. I felt trapped, and in bliss. "I. Love. You. Jade. Uh. This. My. Pussy. Tell me, ma. Tell me!"

Clap. Clap. Clap.

"Uh! It's. Yours. It's. Yours! Bentley! Aw shit, baby. It's yours!" I tried to get free from his hold, but there was no use. His biceps bulged. His weight rested on the back of my thighs, and all I could do was accept the constant pounding of his penis going in and out of me, hitting every untouched region of my womb, until I came, screaming his name.

He came seconds later, sucking on my sweaty neck. Then, he was sucking my breasts, after rolling me on top of him, forcing me to ride him slowly. From this position I felt totally in control. I grabbed the headboard and rode him like a jockey. His lips trapped my nipples and sucked, pulled and sucked some more. Bentley was infatuated with my breasts. He was always squeezing them, or asking me to suck them. I didn't know why, but his fascination with them was becoming a turn on for me. I popped my hips as fast as I could, slamming my womb on his piece. "Shit, Bentley. Shit. I'm cumming, baby. I'm cumming again."

He grabbed my waist and continued to make me slam down on him at full speed. Then he growled. "Argh. Argh. Shit baby. Shit." I could feel him cumming deep within my channel in big blasts.

I fell on top of him and sucked all over his neck. "I love you, baby. I love you so, so much."

"Love you too, ma. You're my baby."

Chapter 12

Bentley

I pulled the skull cap down over my ears and popped the collar of my bomber jacket as the harsh wind blew into my face and caused my clothes to wave like a flag. It was so cold that my nose, ears, and toes felt frozen. Me and Jade were once again on top of the Peter McGuire Housing Projects. And, we were in the second course of her training. I had five dogs hung upside down by their legs. All were fighters and had lost their bouts and were on their way out of the game. Instead of allowing the homies of Camden to slice their throats like they did most of the loser dogs, I snatched them up and brought them to the roof, so Jade could get used to killing shit.

She stood a few feet away, with her pants wagging in the harsh wind. Her scarf blew as well. She had on a pair of purple Uggs that matched her Fendi jacket I'd gotten her for the New Year.

I stepped beside her. "Aiight, baby. It's twenty-nineteen. A new year. From this day forward, I need your heart to be as cold as your husband's. I need you to hate before you love. See the bad in everything until you find the good. And never hesitate to pop this cannon. Fall in love with the sound of the blasts. When your ears ring, let it remind you of the power you hold over life and death. You got me?"

She nodded. "I gotchu." She glanced at the targets. "Which one am I hitting first?"

I stood behind her and kissed her cold cheek. I nibbled on her earlobe and slipped my tongue into it. "You can murder any one you want to, just as long as you take each one of them out. This long leg hanging out of the handle is an extended clip. You got thirty shots in it. Make 'em count." I slid my hands around hers and got ready to raise the gun with her

She pushed back on my chest. "N'all, I got this. I don't need no help." She aimed. "They tried to attack you, right baby? Went for your throat and all of that?"

I nodded as the smoke from the cold weather came from my mouth. "Hell yeah, they did, boo. They tried to kill your hubby. Lights out, ma."

She ran her tongue across her pearly whites. "Yeah, baby, it's lights out." Aimed and pulled the trigger.

Boom. Boom. Boom.

Her bullets ripped into the animals' flesh, left big holes inside of them. She fired ten more shots, walking up closer to her targets and hitting them all, and then going down the line again, shooting until her clip was empty.

All of the animals swung back and forth with blood dripping from them. Their tongues were like cords hanging from their mouths. Smoke rose from her pistol. The heavy scent of gunpowder wafted into the air. It smelled so sweet, that all I could do was smile.

I ran over to her and wrapped her in my arms, picked her up. "That's what I'm talkin' about, baby. That's my li'l one right there. Now you ready to move on."

She wrapped her arms around my neck before tonguing me down. "I just wanna ride wit you baby. I just wanna ride beside my hubby until my last breath. That's all that matters to me. Until the end of time. That's it."

I cuffed that big ass booty, and tongued my lady down, falling more and more crazy, and obsessively in love with her.

The next two days were more of the same thing. It got to the point that Jade was hungry to murder. She started to walk around with the motel with the .380 in her hand like it was a purse or something. I found that shit to be so attractive. Every time I couldn't help myself from snatching her up and taking her down. I loved eating that pussy while she held both of my guns in her hands. Telling me to eat her faster and swallow her juices. She was slowly becoming the female version of me. A version I could cherish and love.

***

She and I both went over to Guns' apartment in the Peter McGuire Projects two days later. When he answered the door, he was in a pair of boxers and smelled like loud pussy. He had a big smile on his face as usual. His forehead was wet with sweat. "Y'all come on in here. I'm just finishing up some shit wit my baby girl." He stepped into the house, and we followed close behind. "Excuse the presentation of the place."

I kept Jade a few inches behind me. I didn't know what to expect, and if I'd seen anything out of the ordinary, I would have turned around and got us out of there. The first thing I saw was the same yella female from a week ago. She stood on the side of the couch with her breasts spilling over the top of her bra. From the waist down, she was naked. Her hand roamed up and down her crease. Her eyes connected with mine. She smiled and licked her lips. "Daddy, they coming to play wit us?" she asked, now sizing up Jade.

"Hell n'all. This ain't that type of party," Jade responded before Guns had the chance to. She tightened her grip on my arm and mugged the yellow broad with anger.

Guns laughed, but I ain't see shit funny. "Yo, shorty shut that shit down right away. What's really good though?" He took ahold of her hand and lowered his head to kiss the back of it.

She yanked it away from him and pushed him so hard, he stumbled backward. "I don't know you like that to be kissing or touching me," she snapped.

He fell against the door and bounced up from it. Lowered his eyes and made his way in our direction. "Man, who the fuck this bitch think she talking to?"

Jade nudged me aside and pulled out her .380. Cocked it, and aimed it directly toward his face, after pulling back the hammer.

I blocked his path, with a scowl placed over my mug. Heart pounding in my chest and ready to kill over my rib. He bumped into me with his naked chest. I could smell the funk of his sex act, mixed with the alcohol on his breath. "Guns, I fuck wit you but if you think you about to put yo hands on my wife, nigga on everything, I'm finna kill you and that red bitch. This ain't that, Blood. Word up."

He stopped, mugged Jade, then trailed his eyes up to mine. Ma kept her pistol trained on him. Her nostrils flared. Her eyelids were low. I could tell she was ready to pop him or any other nigga, for that matter. Her heart was turning as cold as the weather outside and that was making me more possessive of her.

Guns swallowed. "I been knowing you since we were kids, Bentley. We done fucked a few hoes together. We ain't never let pussy come between us. But, this how you feel, though?" he snapped, walking around me.

I placed my hand on top of Jade's pistol. "It's good, baby. He ain't mean nothing by it. Put it away," I ordered her.

She kept her eyes on him, and slowly fixed her pistol from firing ready, before she replaced it. "Yo, don't nobody put they hands on me, but him. I don't know you like that."

Guns picked up a bottle of Patrón from the table and turned it up, guzzling like a thirsty whale or something. He lowered the bottle and burped loudly. "Yo, this gotta be shorty that you kept referring to as your rib, huh? The li'l one you been taking up to the roof to kill them pussies that lost their fights?"

The high yella girl had backed all the way up to the hallway. She looked confused and as if she didn't know whether to come back into the living room, or to run into the bedroom and hide.

"Yeah. This my baby right here. Her name Jade."

Jade cleared her throat. "No, excuse him. I'm his wife and yes, my name is Jade. I heard a lot about you, Guns. It's nice to finally meet you." She held out her hand for him to shake.

He looked down at it, then came around the couch and shook it. Laughed. "Yo, she is bad though, bruh. I gotta give you that. Damn, I forgot how Brooklyn bred dimes. That's my bad, shorty, for overstepping my bounds. But, damn, you cold. Your swag terrific too. I like that killa shit."

She pulled her hand back and stepped on the side of me, slid her arm around the small of my back. "Baby, how long we finna be over here?"

I sat down on the couch and pulled her down with me. "Not that long, I just wanna see what kid got for me. I looked over to Guns as he settled onto the love seat across from us. The redbone made her way across the room to sit on his lap. Once there, she straddled his lap with her back to us. She peppered kisses along his neck.

"Yo, can we talk bidness wit ya Earth right there, son?" he asked, nodding his head over at Jade.

"Yeah, it's good," I replied and squeezed Jade's hand lightly. I could tell she ain't wanna be in those projects. Her body language told me she was uncomfortable. I didn't like seeing her like that.

"Son, I got a ten-thousand-dollar lick for you that I can't hit. Let's just say it's a conflict of interest. I can't go no deeper than that. But, anyway, it should be real easy."

I scooted forward on the couch. The leather pillows ruffled under me. "What I'm doing? Popping something, or sending them on they way? Either way, it don't matter to me." Ten gees sounded real good to me. I could add it with the seventy-five hundred I already had stashed in the motel room. I would need about fifteen thousand more before I thought me and Jade would have enough paper to set out on our own, away from the East Coast, where we were hotter than charcoals in a grill pit.

Guns looked over to Jade. "You sho she good, bruh?"

"Yo, what about that broad in your lap? Is that bitch good?" I snapped, getting heated. I ain't know that yella bitch from Adam. For all I knew, she could be a snitch. She seemed real naïve and young-minded.

Guns grinned and nodded, gripped her big ass and rubbed all over it. "Yeah, my bitch good. She knows if she repeats anything that happen around daddy, I'll slay her whole family, before I slice her throat. Ain't that right, li'l baby?"

She rose from sucking on his neck and rubbed the back of his head. "That's right. I'd never open my mouth anyway, daddy. Unless it's to fill it with this." She reached between their bodies and grabbed his piece.

"Yo, y'all can't wait to we leave to do all of that stuff? I mean, damn. It's highly inappropriate." Jade frowned.

This seemed to ignite the passion in the yella broad. She moaned as she sucked on Guns' neck. "I'll fuck you in front of them, daddy. I'll show them how we really get down. You know I will."

He laughed. "Anyway. You ain't gon be doing shit, but hitting this nigga that's coming into town. Real simple. He coming into town thinking he finna receive a package, but ain't shit happening. The only thing he gon receive is slugs. The homies say when he get out the way, it's gon open up a whole market for the dope boys. He the only holdout that's cock blocking the flood right now. So, he gotta eat them bullets, nah mean?"

I shrugged my shoulders. "Fuck 'em. When this shit set to go down, and when do I get paid?"

The yella bitch rose up, and slipped on to his piece. Threw her head back and moaned. "Oh, daddy. Yes! Yes! Fuck." She groaned, moving up and down on him.

Guns clenched his teeth and held her ass. "Wait. Wait. Hold on baby." He lifted her off of his dick and stood up. He walked to the back room and came back and tossed me a knot of money. "That's ten gees right there. I'll let you know when the nigga get into town. We'll go from there. Oh, and Santana gon be calling you tonight. He say he got that bread. I'd tell you to call him, but he switching phones, trying to avoid them alphabet boys. He did say he'll get up with you tonight though."

He walked back over to the love seat where the yella bitch was rubbing her pussy and smushing her lips together. She pulled her bra under her breasts again. The nipples were rock hard. Guns picked her up and slid her back on to his dick. "I don't know how much he owe you, but a deal is a deal. Don't let that be the reason you forfeit this mission. If you walk out of here with that cheese, that means we're on. It's as simple as that."

I felt offended. Grabbed Jade's hand and pulled her up. "Nigga, don't disrespect me like that in front of my queen. I know how the game go. I ain't new to this shit. I'ma handle my bidness on both ends. Just hit my phone when it's good."

The redbone started to bounce up and down at full speed, moaning loudly. I watched their sexes work over each other's and could smell their scent. It turned my stomach. The whole scene was gross to me.

"We good then. I'll. I'll. Fuck wit you later. Uh. Fuck." Guns groaned, bouncing her up and down.

Jade pulled me. "Let's go, baby. Let's get the hell out of this project building." She turned her nose up and mugged the fucking pair before we parted.

***

"Don't ever bring me back around no shit like that again, Bentley. That was fucking disgusting!" she snapped as we drove the hype's rental car out of the parking lot of the projects. Guns had worked out a deal with one of his hypes that had a few cars. That allowed me and Jade to rent his Nissan Maxima for a week at a time. The car was clean and rolled smoothly.

"Baby, that's bad. I ain't know that nigga was gon have that thirsty young bitch over there all over him like that. Bruh was probably off a pill and using her for her box, that's all."

Jade sat back in the passenger's seat. "You been going over there a lot since we been in Jersey. I hope you ain't fucked that bitch. She definitely had her eyes on you like she was lusting." She rolled down her window, spit out of it and rolled it back up. "So, did you?"

I kept rolling, before frowning at her. "You talking stupid. Shut that shit up."

I ain't feel like getting into no huge argument with her. I had too much on my mind.

"Nigga, that ain't a no. Answer my question? You ever screwed that li'l girl or not?"

"N'all! Now don't ask me that shit no more. I ain't fucked wit nobody since I been wit you. That's it, that's all. Damn." She mugged the side of my head because I refused to look at her for fear of our argument lasting longer than it should have. "Yo, you better watch ya tongue with me, Bentley. I'm ya queen, not them other hoes. Check yaself."

I bit into my bottom lip and tried to keep calm. I ain't wanna snap on my rib, but she was testing my gangsta. "Yeah, aiight, ma."

She scoffed and let her seat back. "Nigga, you belong to me. Period."

Chapter 13

Jade

"Baby, seriously. Why we gotta come in here? I feel like I'm about to burn up or something," Bentley said, creeping into the big church as if he were waiting for a bunch of angels to swoop down and attack him for all of the wrongs he'd done. It was so funny that I couldn't help laughing at him. "Then you laughing and shit. Yo, this foul, Jade."

It was the same day that we'd visited Guns and he'd gotten the ten-thousand-dollar contract. For some reason, when we were on our way past the church, it had called out to my heart. I needed to be inside of it. So, I'd made him stop the car after seeing a pastor come out of the church getting ready to lock the doors. I'd yelled out to him to hold fast, and thankfully he had. He opened the doors and we introduced ourselves, before he agreed to allow me and Bentley to come inside so we could pray. I asked him for another favor as well and was overjoyed when he agreed to that as well. I was so excited. I knew it would catch Bentley off guard.

"Baby, I'm not laughing at you. I'm laughing with you. Now come in before the pastor change his mind," I ordered, reaching out my hand for him.

He stepped into the door and looked around as if he were super paranoid. "Yo, I'll only stay for a minute. I ain't tryna get burned up or nothing. Pretty sure I ain't welcome in here." He took my hand and eased inside.

I led him to one of the back pews and walked until we got into the middle of it, then pulled him down. "Look, you're married now. That means that you have to step over to my side of the fence here and there as well. Now, my heart called me to come here so I could pray, and I want to pray over you as well. Come on."

He looked up toward the ceiling. "Yo, I don't believe in all that mystical stuff. God ain't checking for people like us, Jade, unless he trying to strike us down with lightning." He continued to scan the ceiling of the church.

It was taking all of my patience to not laugh and snap out at him. "Dang, Bentley, you'll believe He'll do all of that bad stuff to you, and in your mind that makes him real. But, when it comes to believing He'll hear our prayers, then it's all about mystics?" I rolled my eyes. "Boy, hush and bow your head."

I waited for him to do so. Pastor Evans stood in the far distance closer to the pulpit. He smiled at me and crossed his self with the sign of the cross. I did the same thing, before closing my eyes, taking Bentley's hands into mine. "Our Father, who art in heaven, Father in the mighty name of Jesus, we ask that You hear our prayers and praise. Father we ask for Your cleansing. We know we've done a lot of wrong and have hurt a bunch of people, but we ask that You forgive us of our sins, and that You allow for our marriage to be pure and authentic in only your sights. Entwine our spirits. Make our hearts beat as one and have mercy on our souls. We are lost and need Your guidance. Please bless our beloved family and loved ones. If it is Your will, please allow for us to see them again. If not, please heal our longing for them. Lastly, please forgive us for all of our past, present and future sins. We know there will be many more. In Jesus' holy and precious name, we pray as one flesh and spirit. Amen."

I slowly opened my eyes and looked over at Bentley. His eyes remained closed. He opened the right one and looked toward the top of the church as if he were afraid. Then slowly, his second eye opened after I remained quiet for a while.

"Yo, baby, are you done? Can we get up out of here now?" He damn near jumped out of his skin when Pastor Evans stepped to the side of the pew. "Holy fuck, man. You can't be creeping up on people like that. What's wrong with you?" His hand slid under his coat.

I reached over and covered his mouth with my hand, blushed as I looked up at the pastor. He held a white veil in his hands. "Bentley, shut up. You're not supposed to be swearing in God's house. Have some respect. Sorry, Pastor Evans. He's new at this."

The pastor, a light-skinned, heavyset man with a small afro, smiled. "It's okay, li'l sista. You just take it upon yourself to keep praying over him. The Bible says that a wife can sanctify her husband through her prayers, even if he does not. When the time is right, God will call him. In this day and age, the Lord tends to reach out to the women first, so follow your heart. Now, get on up so I can bless this union."

Bentley shot a confused glance at me as we made our way to a stand. "What he talkin' about, baby?"

I took his hand and led him to the front of the church, where the pastor stood at the ready. I took a deep breath as the Pastor placed a veil over the top of my locks that had grown considerably since me and Bentley had set out on our escapade. After he had it in place, he stepped in front of us and smiled. I turned to Bentley. "Baby, you said you would stand before God and take a vow to be my husband. Pastor Evans has agreed to pray for our union and to send our marriage up to Jehovah. Are you all in?"

He looked over to the pastor, and then to me. "Yo, I don't need to do all that to honor you as my wife. You are mine. I'll go ape shit over you, ma. Word up." He frowned and looked as if he was about to wild out. I saw that murderous look in his eyes, and knew I needed to calm him down. Bentley didn't like surprises. He didn't like things that came out of the blue that put him on the spot.

I stepped forward and held his handsome face in my hands, tilted it downward so he could look into my eyes. "Baby, calm down, and listen to me. Okay?"

He was starting to shake. I knew that meant he was really getting fired up. I wondered if it was because of the pastor that stood a short distance away, with an amused look on his face. "Yo, I'm good."

"Baby, right now, this isn't about you. It's about me. I know I am already your wife. I will do anything for you with no hesitation, but sending it up to Jehovah will be everything for me. So please, baby, just do this for me."

He tilted his head backward and exhaled, continued to look at the ceiling, before eventually peering into my eyes. "Damn you. Baby, what I gotta do?"

I smiled and rubbed the side of his face. "Just let the pastor pray over us, and say what comes from your heart when it's your turn to say your vows. Can you do that?"

He nodded. "I can."

The pastor came and stood in front of us again. "Dearly beloved, we are gathered here today to bring together both sister Jade, and..."

Bentley raised his head. "Bentley."

The Pastor's eyes got big. He looked Bentley over real close. He seemed to be transfixed for a second, then shook it off. "...Bentley, in holy matrimony. Father in the mighty name of Jesus, we ask that you bless this union. Bring these two young hearts together and help your Will to be done in their lives." He cleared his throat twice and stopped. When I looked up at him, he appeared to be shaking. Sweat slid down the side of his face, and the church was as cool as a spring day. Something wasn't right.

"Pastor, are you okay?"

He jumped. "Huh? Uh, yeah, li'l sister. I just, uh. Well, where were we? Oh yeah. Bentley, do you take Jade to be your wife? Will you have her, hold her, protect, sanctify, and bless her through sickness and in health as long as you both shall live?" The pastor was shaking so bad, his knees were knocking into each other.

"Yo, what's wrong wit you, Dunn? You gotta piss a something?" Bentley asked, curling his top lip.

"N'all, I'm just cold. I-I-I got thin blood. My—"

"Baby, just answer the question. Please."

"Hell, yeah, I do. This my rib. I'ma hold her down until the death of me, word to Jehovah, man," Bentley said with pride and mounting suspicion.

"Okay now, Pastor, ask me. Hurry up," I urged.

The Pastor's face was dripping sweat. His underarms looked as if they were peeing. "Uh, and do you Jade take Bentley, to be your husband before Jehovah? Will you have him, hold, him, be loyal to him, and be his helper as long as the both of you shall live?"

"I won't be his helper, I'll be his equal, but I agree to everything else for as long as I live. That's on my soul."

"Before I sanctify this marriage, would either of you like to say anything?" the pastor asked.

Bentley mugged him from the corners of his eyes. I could tell he was hip to him. His nostrils flared off and on. He clenched his teeth. He looked as if he was seconds away from going off.

"N'all, Pastor, that's it. Sanctify us. Hurry up."

He was shaking so bad he could barely stand up. "Okay, by the powers invested in me through our Lord and Savior Jesus Christ, I now pronounce you husband and wife. You may kiss your bride."

Bentley snatched me to him and tongued me down. The whole time, he never took his eyes off of the pastor. As soon as our kiss finished, he reached past me and snatched the Reverend up with both hands, held him high off of his feet. "What the fuck is the matter? You know me from somewhere?"

I rushed this back. "Baby. Put him down. Put him down, and let's get out of here," I hollered.

"Fuck that. Where you know me from? Spit it out!" He shook the man and tightened his grip on his suit jacket.

"From-m-m-m the n-n-news. Both of y'all. Cop killers. Armed and dangerous." he stuttered.

"Fuck!" Now he had me cursing in church. "Just let him go and we gon get out of here, baby. Come on."

"Hell n'all, if I let this fool go, he'll have every policeman in Jersey looking for our ass. We can't risk it, Jade. I gotta smoke him."

"No! Please, young man! Aw, Lord! Help me! Help me now, Lord!"

Bentley pulled out a Glock, pressed it to the man's forehead and cocked the hammer. "Baby, go wait in the car. Hurry up, I'll be out in a minute."

I almost crapped myself. "Baby, no. He's a man of God. You can't. Please." I begged, fearing the worst for the pastor.

"Jade, go wait in the fuckin' car! I ain't gon tell you again! Go!" he shouted, with anger written across his face. His eyes were red as fire.

I backed away. "Baby, please, let's just go. Please don't kill him. I'm begging you." Tears came out of my eyes. I continued to walk backward.

"It's the only way, Jade. Fuck him. Your heart gotta be cold! I told you that!" he yelled, stabbing a knife through my heart with each decibel. I hated when Bentley screamed at me. Made me feel both angry and hurt at the same time.

"Baby, please don't. My heart is cold, but he's a man of God. We can't." More tears dripped from my eyes, and down my cheeks. I was seconds away from throwing up.

"Fuck, Jade! Only for you! Only for my muthafuckin' rib!" He smacked him across the chin with the gun and knocked him out cold. Mugged me, then drug him into the second pew and left him there. Come on, let's get the fuck out of here."

***

Later that night, we sat a big sausage and pepperoni pizza in the middle of the bed, and ate it in silence. We'd been back to the motel for three hours and neither he nor I had said a word to each other. I felt sicker than I did back in the church when I was sure he was going to kill the pastor. I tried to get engrossed in the sitcom we watched on the motel's television. But, I couldn't, my mind was wandering like crazy. I had to know what was going through his brain. It wasn't like him to be spent for so long when we were together. I wondered if he was having second thoughts about us. And, if so, what should my next move be? I questioned if I was strong enough to make it on my own. Maybe I wasn't cut out to be a goon's wife. Maybe I was too soft.

He picked up a slice, bit off of it, and put it back down, wiped his mouth with a napkin, and grabbed the remote control, flipping through the channels. He grabbed his grape soda and took a long drink from it.

I could no longer take the silence. "Baby, say something. All of this silence is starting to piss me off and make me think some crazy thoughts. If you ain't messin' wit me no more, then just say it. Damn."

He flipped through the channels some more, then lowered the remote with a smile on his face. Before I could turn to the television to see what he was smiling at, he turned up the volume as loud as it could go.

I snapped my neck to look at the television as I heard the familiar voice of the pastor. "Then the man grabbed me by my neck, and he put his gun right here in my forehead and said, 'I gotta Ooo him, Jade.' No wait, he said, 'I gotta smoke him, Jade.' Yeah, that's what he said. And pressed that big ol gun harder into my forehead and I hollered out to the Lord. I said, Lord, if you listening save me. Save me from Satan himself 'cause he sho nuff about to send me up yonder. If I'da known I was gone run into Satan and his wife today, I would have stayed home, or even better, I'da never left Arkansas to begin with. Have mercy. And they are just like y'all said, armed and dangerous."

The Asian reporter stepped away from the pastor and our pictures appeared on the screen. "If you see these two, do not approach them. They are very armed and very dangerous. If they can do something as grotesque as this to a member if the church, then... Well, God help us all. Reporting live from the corner of Thirty-Sixth Avenue, I am—"

Bentley turned off the television and grunted. "Now we gotta hit it from here. Thanks a lot." He slid out of the bed and walked into the bathroom.

I followed behind him. "You're blaming this on me? Really? Because I didn't wanna see you kill some preacher?"

He pulled out his dick, pulled up the toilet seat, and began to piss, finished and replaced the lid before washing his hands. "Had I smoked dude bitch ass, nobody would have known we were in Jersey. But now, this bitch just as hot has New York. Damn, Jade. I should a went with my first mind. We didn't need him to validate our union no way. The same mafucka that married us is the same one that ran to the law. Bitch-nigga."

I grabbed his mouth and held it. "Bentley, you gon learn to watch how you be talking around me. All that cursing ain't necessary. I am your queen. Speak to me with seasoned words. You got that?"

He knocked my hand away and bumped me to get out of the close confines if the bathroom. Watched me from the corners of his eyes the whole time. "Yeah, I hear you. But I also heard that preacher too." He flopped on the bed. "Next time let me do my thing, aiight? Fuck everybody except us, Jade. You understand me?"

I nodded. "Yeah." I went over and set beside him. "So now what? Are you regrettin' marrying me?"

He was silent while he looked me over. "Never that. I got the baddest bit..." He caught himself. "Queen in the world," then laughed.

"Yeah, you better check yourself."

He laughed. "Get up here." He pulled on me until I was straddling him and kissed my lips. "I love you, boo."

I smiled. "I love you too." Kissed him again. "So now what?"

"Well, we gon..." His phone started to vibrate. "Hold up." He pulled it out, and looked over the face. "Yo, this Santana punk ass. I gotta take this, baby. Give me a second." He moved me from off of him and stood up. "Nigga, what's good wit my paper?"

He stepped out of the room and I continued to watch the news with the sound off. The breaking news in red at the bottom of the screen was freaking me out. They had all sorts of pictures of both me and Bentley at various different stages of our journey. They even posted one of him at the Walmart when he'd bussed a move to get us those few things for the abandoned apartment that we'd stayed in. The sight of him in a wife beater, out in the freezing cold while I'd been back at the apartment with his bomber jacket as warm as I could be, reminded me of how much he truly loved me even before he'd said it. I had a good man. I had to hold him down.

He rushed out of the bathroom. "Yo, we gotta meet up wit Santana. He got my bread. And I gotta have my paper. This nigga done had it long enough. Besides, if he got it, then we can be on our way. Jersey on fire right now any way, fuckin' wit that preacher." He said the last part so low, I could barely hear him. "Come on, let's go get dressed. Unless you gon wait here until I get back? Yeah, why don't you do that?" I bounced off of the bed with the television still playing behind me.

"Where we meeting him at? Because you know you ain't leaving me here, or nowhere else from here on out. This is us."

He sighed and nodded. "Brooklyn."

Chapter 14

Bentley

"Babe, why in the hell would we be meeting this idiot back in New York? This is ridiculous. It just doesn't make sense. We're on fire here." Jade said from the passenger's seat. She'd been getting on my nerves ever since we got on the interstate to head back towards New York. I could tell she was worried and she didn't trust Santana.

"Ma, I hear what you saying, goddess, but I gotta have that paper. It's the only way we ain't gotta stay in Camden, hitting a bunch of senseless ass licks, only to come up with the bare minimum. Them ten thousands at a time take too long to add up, and by the time we get the next one, we'd been on spent most of the one we got before it because doesn't stop going and the cost of living is a bitch. So we gon get this bag from Santana, and then head back to Camden and finish that last move, before we leave this side of the States altogether. Guns getting our identifications and passports right too. I think we gon have to take some new pics soon too. What you think about Cuba? Did you pay attention in Spanish class?" I smiled at her to lighten the mood.

She mugged me, then looked off. "Cuba seems a million miles away, Bentley, especially when in order to get there, you have to roll through the toll taker that is Santana, with his janky ass. I don't trust him as far as I can throw him. My intuitions are telling me that he got something up his sleeve. And why we meeting him when he owe us? That's backwards to me." She exhaled loudly.

The more she talked, the more I started to feel how she was feeling. Santana said the reason why he wanted me to meet him back in Brooklyn was because he had a bunch of shit going down in East New York for the next two days that he had to oversee, and that he absolutely couldn't step away from not even for a minute. He said it would be easier for him if I came and picked up my bag, and rolled back out. I would be lying if I said that my spider senses weren't tingling, but I was so thirsty for my shit that I just had to do what I had to do. I was strapped and ready for any type of blind side, though I didn't know what he could possibly gained from that. I mean, it wasn't like we were enemies or anything like that. If anybody should have been upset by all of the things that had transpired between him and me, it should have been me. I was forced to be the patient one, not him.

"Well?" Jade asked, frowning at me with her lil, pretty, strategically freckled face. There had to be a God because He had most definitely taken His time making her.

"Well what, ma? Damn," I asked, stopping at the toll booth and throwing two rolls of quarters into it. It seemed like they were steady going up in the fee to cross over from Jersey to New York every few weeks. It was ridiculous.

"Well, why are we meeting him, and not the other way around, Bentley? Why are you not asking yourself these questions? We could be walking into a freaking trap. Our rewards are up to a hundred thousand a piece and that's since a few hours ago. You don't think Santana would break his neck to cash in two hunnit thousand dollars? And if not for the money, what if he got into some bull crap and is using us for leverage? Think. Think. Think." She poked at her temple over and over.

"Yo, chill ma. Damn. I thought about all of that shit already, and I don't know what this fool is on, but we need that money. Now, I hate you rolling wit me because I don't know what to expect, but you said you refused to stay back at the motel, so this is where we are. We just gotta be on point. Be prepared for the unknown. It's fucked up, I know. But this is us, right?" I glanced over at her, and placed my hand on her thick thigh, squeezing it.

She was quiet for a moment, kept looking out the window as the snow fell from the sky. Exhaled out loud, then nodded. "Yeah, babe. This is most definitely us. I just hope you know what you're doing. You're still my Adam."

I jerked my head back, confused. "Yo, Adam? Yo, you sayin' I'm your white boy now? What that's supposed to mean?" I asked damn near offended.

She rubbed her forehead, then her temples as if she was getting frustrated. "Now, baby, Adam was the first man created in the Bible. After Jehovah created him, then He created Eve from his rib. Adam was meant to lead and protect Eve. And Eve was created to give birth to the world, but at the same time have her husband's back. I am your Eve. I got your back. But you must be my Adam. You have to lead, and see to it that our path is righteous, or else we will be kicked out of the garden."

I frowned. "Yo, what garden, ma? And why does it feel like you're speaking in riddles?"

She sighed again. "Baby, in the Bible, the garden was one of the seven heavens. Jehovah had designated a whole heaven just for them to populate. He told them that all of it belonged to them, with the exception of one tree. He told them they could eat all the fruits of this heaven, but to stay away from one tree and its apples, but Eve was tricked by a serpent into pursuing the one thing that Jehovah had forbade. Long story short, her and Adam ate of this fruit and were kicked out of the garden. In this case, the garden would be our lives and our freedom."

I nodded. "And the apple would be the seventy-five thousand dollars that we are pursuing. That's our forbidden fruit, right?"

"Exactly. And Santana could possibly be the serpent. We don't know yet, but there is a reason Jehovah gave us women intuition. It's because in the very beginning we were tricked by the devil, and now we are fully equipped to know when something isn't right. We no longer need our Adams, our rib bearers, to make choices for us. We are equally intelligent, and wise."

"Yo, that's why niggas be saying shorty my rib. It's because of your Bible, right Jade?"

"Yeah, I come from your rib. Bentley, but you know what, if you're wrong about trusting Santana, I'ma come for your ass with these sized seven in women Uggs. That's my word." I expected her to laugh, and giggle, but she did none of the such. Instead, she kept a mug on her face. Then reached and hooked her phone up to the car's system. Before long, Ella Mai was crooning out of the speakers.

I sat there rolling with my left hand on the steering wheel. I kept looking from the road, back to Jade. She looked so angry that I knew anything I'd say couldn't do nothing but wind up with us falling into a big argument. She wasn't feeling this journey. That was that. I saw the sign that told me were headed to the borough of Brooklyn. Good ol' East New York.

I had mixed feelings about it. The first feeling was that of paranoia, and the second was a sense of longing for my mother. I'd not called or checked on her ever since Jade and I had been on the run. I worried that the drugs had officially taken her under. Then wondered if that is what had taken place, if that meant that it was my fault, because I'd in a sense neglected her.

I shook my head to release that thought. I had to focus on the task at hand. And protect the queen that set before. My mother was a part of my old world. Jade was the new. I rubbed her thigh again. "Don't worry, baby. We gon be good. Hubby got this. One way or the other." I wanted so desperately for that to be truth. But, the truth was I was just as worried as she was. Our backs were against the wall. Money was the motive.

***

We sat in the car for twenty minutes in silence, inside of Coney Island, waiting for Santana to show up. It looked like there was another winter storm brewing. This was the first month of the New Year and it was taking upon the likes of the wintery December before it. Thick patches of white fell from the sky. And the Nissan Maxima that we rolled, swayed from left to right. Ella Mai continued to croon out of the speakers. Somewhere along the way Jade had snuck her left hand inside of mine and as we sat there in the parking lot it was my first time interlocking my fingers with a female. At first it made me feel soft and kind of weak, I wanted to pull my hand away. But then, the more I looked over at how bad my woman was, and how much we'd been through, I just didn't care about the soft feeling. I just wanted to make her happy.

She kissed the back of my hand and smiled. "Can't wait until we're able to have our own place, where we can be hugged up all day long without a care in the world. Seems like we're always on the move. I'm so tired, Bentley. So, so tired. I just want us to be happy and as far away from here as possible. Being here is making me think about my mother, Ashley, and Ashland. I miss them so much." She lowered her head, and sighed in defeat.

I rubbed her back and was about to do as best as I could to console her when I heard the sound of loud music pounding. The ground began to shake just a bit. I turned around in my seat, to see an all-black Hummer rolling into the parking lot of Coney Island. The bass coming from it was hitting so hard that the windows to our Nissan were rattling. It parked to the right of us.

"That must be Santana shiesty ass right there. He driving a Hummer so he shouldn't have no problem upping that money. He is causing a scene though." She turned around in her seat to see how much attention the big Humvee was drawing to the area.

I slid my hand under my jacket, and gripped the handle of my Glock, ready for the unthinkable. All Red Hook niggas grew to be real cutthroat over time. I didn't think Santana would be no different. "Baby, if I see anything funny I'm splashing this nigga, I'm letting you know that right now."

She nodded. "As you should. It's all about us. Word." She leaned over and kissed my cheek.

Santana opened the door to the big Hummer and jumped out of it, wearing a red and black leather Marc Jacob. He had the matching skull cap with the leather ear straps on it. He stepped in the snow rocking a pair of red and black Timbs. Closed the door and blew into his closed fist. The cold smoke rose from his mouth and glove. He rubbed his gloves together and threw his hands up outside of the car.

I mugged him for a second, then opened the driver's door. The bell that indicated one of the doors of the car was opened started to ding back to back. "Yo, ma, I'll be right back. Let me see what this fool's talking about."

"He shouldn't have nothin' to say. Just hand over that bag," Jade snapped, glaring at him through the window of the passenger's side.

"Yeah, I know, but let me check it out." I got out of the car and headed over to him. The snow began to blow from the ground as the wind picked up. It was seven o'clock at night, and the sun was beginning to set.

He started to walk in my direction. "Yo, what it do, Blood? A nigga ain't seen you in a minute. What's really good?"

I shook up wit him and gave him a half-hug. "Ain't nothing good. Shit been all bad ever since you broke camp wit that lil scratch. Been trying to bounce back ever since then with the Jakes on my ass, kid. Where that bag at?"

He smiled. "Nigga, I got that and a few extra crumbs for you. I bussed a major move. We about to take over New York, Blood. Trust me on that. Let's roll out." He turned and started in the direction of his Hummer but stopped. "Yo, you won't believe who put me in either. Wait to you see this." He turned to get back into the Hummer.

I grabbed his arm. "Hold on, bruh, you mean to tell me you ain't got my shit wit you? Fuck type of shit is that?" I asked, with my heart starting to pound. What the fuck was wrong wit this nigga? And I wondered why he insisted on playing with my bread.

The back doors of the Hummer opened up and two dudes with red bandanas over their faces jumped out of it with MACs in their hands. Santana snatched his arm from me, and held up a hand at them, before waving them off. "Yo it's good. Y'all get on back in the truck this my nigga."

I watched them stare me down for what seemed like an eternity. Then they slowly climbed back into the Hummer and slammed the door. The window rolled down in the back and I noticed the two barrels from the MAC poked out of it on the sneak tip.

Santana smiled. "It's all love, Slime. You knew damn well I wasn't gon bring no seventy-five bands out wit me. It's at the safe house though. All ready to go. Follow me." He pulled open the door, the music boomed out of it. Then he climbed back into his Hummer and closed the door. The scent of loud was heavy in the atmosphere now.

I cursed under my breath. "Here we go with this bullshit."

Chapter 15

Jade

I looked around the big mansion from the couch and felt so uncomfortable. The lights were dimmed. It felt like the heat was turned all the way up. The music blared way too loud. There were dudes walking around with pistols poking out of their shirts and red bandanas hanging out of their pockets, or draped around their necks.

The females were damn near naked. They were all topless and paraded through the mansion in bikini bottoms. Champagne glasses of assorted drinks in their hands. They were laughing and talking so loud that I wanted to smack the shit out of all of them. I saw more than a few tooting heathy lines of cocaine, before pulling their heads back, and grooving to the music while they pinched their nostrils together. There were two dudes and two females in the far corner of the room we were sitting in. The dudes were standing up while what looked like two Spanish females were giving them head in the sloppiest fashions.

Kitty corner from them, there were two more females sticking syringes in their veins, and getting high as the poison would take them. I didn't understand what all of this stuff had to do with us getting our money. It seemed like a smoke screen for something bigger that was at play.

Bentley sat beside me heated. He mugged the whole room. It was like smoke was coming from the top of his head. He leaned into my ear. "If this bitch nigga don't give me our money soon, on everything I love, I'm about to snap. I can't believe this bitch ass nigga had me searched and my pistols removed. That got me vexed, Jade. He supposed to be my mans."

"Screw him, baby. I'm your mans. This is us."

He nodded and sat back on the couch and continued to mug the room. It looked like the party was on the verge of turning into an orgy. Instead of two dudes getting head now, there were eight of them, and three females receiving oral right on the floor a short distance away from us. They were positioned so that their privates faced me and Bentley. I wanted to cover my man's eyes.

I was a bit worried since Santana had Bentley's pistols removed. Now we were at his mercy. I felt that something wasn't right when he first had Bentley searched to begin with. Bentley had gave the security the look of death as they patted him down, and threatened him to murder any one if they dared to touch me, so they hadn't. I was thankful for that.

Santana came from the back room and put a bowl of Tropical Loud on the table in front of us. He placed a box of fifty Cuban cigars next to it. "You muthafuckas gotta roll y'all own shit. That's just that." He laughed. "Mafuckas think I'm their maid. Shid." He sat across from us and licked one of the Cubans that had already been rolled.

Bentley slid to the front of the couch and mugged him with hatred. "Santana, you know how I get down about my cheese. Why the fuck are you playing me like a pussy right now?" he asked, curling his upper lil into a vicious scowl.

Santana looked taken aback. "Damn, bruh. A mafucka just thought you'd like a lil get-together before we got into all of that bidness side of things. It's the least I could do after bouncing on you and leaving you in the lurch like that. I mean, look around. If mafuckas is partying on my dime like this, you know it gotta be good. What happened to you? Me and you used to stay on the same page." He licked the cigar, before lighting it.

128

ЕÀ

I wanted to get up myself and slap him across the face. I didn't like how he was doing my man, didn't like the games at all. I was ready to say something when Bentley beat me to it.

"Yo, god, fuck this party. Fuck these bitches. And fuck these niggas. All I care about is my money. I'll party when I got my shit. So, go get it. I'm tired of playing these reindeer games wit you, nigga. Word!" He stood up with both fists balled, eyeing Santana, ready to pounce.

Two of Santana's security detail came and stood behind the couch that Santana was sitting on, with their hands under their shirts. They gave Bentley the look of death. I assumed they were the same two from earlier outside of Coney Island.

Bentley smacked his lips. "You bitch-ass niggas ain't 'bout that life. My word, either one of you pull a banger out in me again without shooting, I'ma murder you and every muthafucka bearing your last name. Now try me! What!" He slid his hand under his shirt and must have forgotten he was without a pistol. His eyes got bucked, as he searched his waist then sighed in defeat after coming up empty.

Santana stood up. "Yo, y'all fall back. Me and my mans about to go upstairs and handle some bidness. Make sure nobody come through those doors. The party is locked. Nobody get in and nobody gets out until three in the morning. Got that?"

The men nodded and went to post up in front of the door. The party continued to go on as if they were oblivious. Now there were nine pairs of people fucking, and sucking. And a whole list of drug users. The scent of the party was also starting to change from that of heavy perfume and weed smoke, to another stench of sex, cigarette smoke, and primos, which were blunts mixed with cocaine and weed.

"Shall we, Bentley?" Santana waved his hand toward the spiral staircase that led up the stairs of the mansion. "Let's go handle this bidness."

Bentley reached for my hand. "Yeah, muthafucka, we shall. Let's get this shit over with." He interlocked our fingers.

Santana mugged our hands, then looked up at me. "Yo, no bitches upstairs, unless they are a part of this grand scheme of things. She gotta wait down here while us men handle bidness. No exceptions."

Bentley bumped him out of the way. "Nigga, watch yo mouth. This my queen. I ain't gon tell you again."

I mugged him on my way past and followed Bentley up the stairs. Santana rushed up them and in front of us to lead the way. The upstairs was full of white carpet. It was quiet up here, and very clean. When we came to the top of the flight, we were met with a hallway that had four doors along it. Santana continued to puff on the blunt, big clouds of smoke drifting to the ceiling. "Yo, Bentley. On everything, I never thought I'd see the day when you'd let a female pussy whip yo ass, especially not a sista. All yo hoes been Spanish and bad. You falling off, kid. Need to let the homie put you back on yo square. Word up. We been niggas since the beginning. Since kids, yo."

"Santana, kids are supposed to turn into men. That's what I am. Fuck your opinions. My bread, Blood. What's good wit it?"

Santana got to the end of the hallway, turned right and opened the door to a den, holding it for us to walk through, which we did. We stepped into the dimly lit room. Inside was a couch, a pool table, and a big armoire. Santana walked over to the armoire and began to push the side of it as hard as he could until it slid across the carpet. Once it was moved enough, he ducked down on the side of it out of view, and I couldn't see what was happening, until a big duffle bag was tossed on the floor. First one, and then another one. "Yo, you think I'm tryna play you out of them peanuts, my nigga? This ain't that. I'm in the game now. I'm in, in." He tossed another bag on to the floor, then backed out of the wall. I had to step to the side to see all of that. There was some sort of trap door in the wall that the armoire had been blocking. He stood straight up and dusted his clothes off. Knelt down and unzipped one of the bags. Grabbed out eight rubber band knots and tossed them at Bentley's feet. "Huh, nigga. That's eighty gees. That extra five on me, baby. Take that petty ass cheese and get the fuck out my mansion. You and this bitch before I get mad. Good luck on the run too, sucka fa love ass nigga." he spat, mugged me, and then Bentley.

Bentley sucked his teeth. "Nigga, you know if I had my piece, I'd take both of them bags and expose that bitch in you. The smartest thing you ever did was take my bangers." He knelt down and picked up the money and handed it to me.

I stuffed it in my purse and zipped it back. That was eighty gees, so my bag looked deformed, but I was happy we had it. I didn't know what Santana had done to come up on the paper, and I didn't care. We had what was ours. It was time to get up out of there.

Santana stood up, reached behind the armoire and came back with a .45 automatic in his hand. "Nigga, what the fuck you just say?" He cocked it, held it at his side.

Bentley stepped in front of me and shielded me away from him. "Yo, you heard what I said, Blood. You been testing my patience a lot on some real shit. You must forget that I get down for the dirty too, nigga. That Red Hook shit in me too. Word up."

Santana raised the gun. "You know what, fuck you, nigga. The latest I checked, it was two hunnit gees on your head. One put up by the law and another one put up by Milan's people. After all, you did whack shorty in cold blood. That hunnit thousand is for your ass and they don't care if you're breathing or dead. Yeah, I think I need that."

Bentley backed up, and took me a few steps with him. "I'll tell you what. I'ma let you turn me in, but just let my shorty leave with that bread and I'm yours."

I felt like I wanted to throw up from even imagining something like that transpiring. "No, baby. Please. Let's just give him the money back, and we'll be on our way. We don't need his stuff no way." I unzipped the purse.

Santana laughed. "Bitch, they got a hunnit racks on yo head too. That's three hunnit gees, and I could use your situation to spring me from a few jams I'm in, in the state of New York. Hell yeah, that sound like a plan to me."

"You's a snake-ass nigga. Straight serpent. But, I shoulda known. I should have known not to trust you," Bentley snapped. "Let her go and take me. She ain't got shit to do wit this," he snapped.

Santana frowned. "What is it about this lil bitch? She fine, but she ain't all that. Ever since she been in the picture, you been acting like a straight simp." He sucked his bottom lip. "It gotta be that pussy then, huh?" He looked me up and down. "Yeah, well after I smoke yo punk ass, I'm finna get me a shot of that. Move that bitch out the way and take these slugs like a man." He held the gun out, and turned his face into a ball of anger. "Now."

"Nigga, you ain't said shit." Bentley pushed me as hard as he could toward the open door. "Go, baby, get out of here. This shit ain't got nothing to do with you!" I fell to the floor of the hallway and he threw his arms out. "Kill me, bitch nigga. Pull that mafuckin' trigger, nigga. Kill me now!"

Santana smiled. "With pleasure." Pulled back the hammer and placed his finger around the trigger.

"Nooooooo!" I hollered, pulling the .380 out of my purse and firing back to back. The shells hopped out of the gun. Slug after slug entered into Santana's body, knocking him into the armoire. He dropped the blunt and slid down until he was sitting on his ass. His eyes were wide open. Blood spilled out of his torso.

Bentley's eyes were buck. He looked down to Santana, and then back to me. There was a thick gray smoke coming from the barrel of my gun. The room was lit with gunpowder. "How the fuck you get through wit that?" he asked, looking back down to Santana.

Tears ran down my cheeks. Holy fuck. I'd just killed somebody. Just killed Santana, it seemed surreal. I struggled to get to my feet. The room felt like it was spinning. "They never searched me, remember? You snapped before they could. Baby, he was finna. I mean, he had his. I'm sorry, I just..."

Bentley raised his foot and stomped Santana in the chest as hard as he could. "Fuck that nigga. Come on, grab this bag." He tossed me one of the duffle bags, picked up Santana's gun and then the other bag. "Let's go out the back."

As we were making our way out of the hallway, one of Santana's security guards came up the stairs with his hand under his shirt. The hallway had speakers at the top of the ceiling of it so the loud music could be heard upstairs. When he got to the top of the landing, he pulled his gun from his shirt. "Hey, what the fuck going on up here?"

Bentley pulled me behind him and fired.

Boom. Boom. Boom.

The hallway lit up with each blast. The bullets slammed into the dude and knocked him back down the steps. I could hear him tumbling down each one of them.

Santana grabbed my hand and we headed down the stairs and out of the back door, and out into the cold winter night with the party blasting behind us.

Chapter 16

Bentley

"Ah! Ah! Ah! No, please. I'm so sorry. I'm so sorry!" Jade screamed, jerking out of her sleep.

I rushed to her side, and snatched her up. "Jade, it's gone be okay, baby. It's finna be okay. You're just going through the remorseful process of taking a life. This will pass," I assured her. Rocking her in my arms and rubbing her back.

This was the third night in the row she'd awakened in screams, all because of Santana's murder. I knew exactly what she was going through. The first time I'd ever taken a life, I went through the same things for a week real bad, and for a month straight I woke up in cold sweats after being terrorized by nightmares that surrounded the murder. It was crazy, and it happened with almost everyone. I just got used to it and no longer allowed the dreams to get the better of me. I knew it was going to be a serious problem for her because she'd known Santana. I'd never had to smoke anybody I really knew, so I could only imagine what she was experiencing with it being her first time, and the fact that she actually knew the person. I felt empathetic. That nigga Santana had to go though. She had to take his ass out and if she didn't, I was sure that he would have laced me right there in front of her, before taking advantage of her in every way he wanted to for the duration of that night.

She buried her face into my chest. Sobbing. Shaking. "I just want him to go away, Bentley. I just want him to go away. I didn't wanna do it. Lord knows I didn't want to," she cried.

I rubbed her back, and planted kisses on the side of her forehead, and cheek. "It's okay, baby. It's okay. This is just the process. Soon it'll be all over. Everything will be better.

We just have to get through this part. And I'm right here to hold you down, ma. I ain't going nowhere. I got you. I got you, boo."

She wrapped the sleeves of my shirt into her small hand and sobbed harder. "Read, baby. Can you read my verse to me over and over? Please, baby." She asked this, looking up to me.

I nodded. "Yeah, ma, I got you." Nudged her head back onto my chest, reached past her and grabbed the Bible off of the night table. Opened it, and flipped through the pages until I got to the book of John. Flipped to the third chapter, and slid my finger down the words. "The sixteenth verse, right baby?"

"Yes, baby. Read it. Please. I need to hear it." She shook some more.

I cleared my throat. Cradled her and kissed her cheek. "Okay, precious. It says that for God so loved the world that He gave His only begotten son. That whosoever should believe in Him shall never perish, but have everlasting life." I rubbed her soft cheek. "That means that as long as you believe in Him, baby, you are going to be okay. You'll live forever and never die. So, you never have to worry. Do you want me to read it again?"

"Yes. Please."

I did. I read it repeatedly, until she fell back to sleep in my arms. The sounds of her light snoring were comforting to my heart. In my eyes she's sacrificed her soul for me. Took another man's life in order to save my own, and in doing so she'd fully conquered me. I loved Jade. She was my Eve like her Bible taught, my rib, my one. That perfect creation that God above had created for me. I was thankful for her and knew I would go to the ends of this world for her. Never in my life had I felt such a way about a woman before. I needed her, and

I would do anything to protect, and keep her happy. She deserved only the best and it was up to me to make sure she had exactly that.

That night, Jade woke me up at four in the morning. She was sitting on the edge of the bed, watching the latest world news that had our story on it. "Baby, look. They got us on the world news now. They just added Santana's murder to the overall body count. Our reward is up to a hundred and fifty thousand a piece, and they've released my mother from jail. Do you think it means she's gotten my sisters back?" she asked, with her little hand on my chest, stroking the scar over my heart.

I got up and scooted behind her. Placed a leg on each side of her, and pulled her blouse over her head to expose the scars along her back. I ran my fingers over them, then kissed them one at a time. "It could, baby. Why, what are you thinking?" I asked, kissing all over her back now, and rubbing my face along the warm skin. Her scent was overwhelming even though it was faint. Jade had my nose wide open. I was taken by her. Now that she'd shed blood on my behalf, it was like I was seeing her in a whole different light. I was becoming obsessed with my queen, and I didn't know how to control that.

"Mmm, that feels good. It's been a few weeks since you've catered to my back, baby. It feels so, so good." She purred and leaned her head all the way forward, smiling for the first time in nearly four days. "Oh, but no, I wasn't really thinking anything. I guess I was just wondering if that meant they'd release my sisters out of foster care. I mean, I know my mother isn't the greatest person in the world, but I'd rather for them to be with her, instead of any other random family or person. They are really beautiful girls and New York, much like the rest of the world, is pretty sick. I shudder at the thought of them winding up with some perverts, or only God knows who." She sighed and leaned her head to the right side.

I sucked on her neck, then sucked along the length of her back, taking my time to lick certain portions of it, before trailing my hands around and cuffing her perfect breasts. I just loved the feel of them, their weight, texture, everything. Jade was perfect. "I feel you, baby. I know it's kind of hard not to think about them. I'm here to talk whenever you want to. I hope you know that, ma." I pulled her head back by her locks and sucked harder on her neck. She had a real thick vein right on the left side. My tongue traced it. Then, I scraped at it with my teeth.

"Mmm. Bentley. It feels so good." She arched her back, then scooted into my chest more closely. I kept on sucking, my left hand in her panties now. "Uh, baby, now that we got the two hundred thousand dollars, where are we gonna go? And when will we leave?" she asked, spreading her thighs further apart to give me better access.

My fingers traced her sex lips, before one slid into her hot pink. She moaned and arched her back, then humped forward into the digit. Her kitty was already dripping wet. Very seldom have I ever touched her there and not found it to be sticky. She had the essence of a true goddess, always on the ready.

"Guns said he about a day out from having all of the proper identifications and passports we'll need to get out of here. I'm thinking Cuba, Jade. Go down there and start a whole new life. I just wanna spoil you until my dying day. Just me and my wife, man, I love you so much." I pulled the finger out and sucked it into my mouth, savored her juices that were on it, then slid my hand back into the center of her thighs, and slid two fingers into her valley, working them in and out. She felt like a silk furnace.

She threw her head all the way back, and sucked on my neck, nibbled on my earlobe. "I love when you call me your wife, baby. I just love to hear it. Makes me feel so special. So complete." Her tongue traced the skin. "Make me cum, Bentley. Now. Do me, baby." She opened her thighs as wide as they could go and placed her right foot on the bed.

I sucked her neck hard. Slid my fingers into her and worked them in and out while my thumb ran circles around her clit. There was a constant sound coming from between her legs. *Sop. Sop. Sop.*

Her cream spilled out of her and dripped onto the bed. I pulled the fingers out and sucked them into my mouth. "Cum for hubby, baby. Cum for me. Got my pussy dripping wet. You know I love feeling this." I pulled my fingers out and spread them apart. The gel was like sticky strings in between my digits. I sucked them into my mouth, then slid them back into her and began to work them in and out at full speed. *Sop. Sop.* Then more twirling my thumb around her clit that drove her crazy.

She humped forward faster and faster. "Uh. Uh. Baby. Baby." She fell back against my chest. Closed her eyes tight and opened her mouth wide. "Un, I don't wanna think about it no more! Uh. Uh. Uh." She placed her hands on the side of the bed, humping faster and faster. "I don't wanna see his face, baby. Just leave me alone! Leave me alone, Santana!" Tears came down her beautiful face.

I sped up my movements, going as deep as the gates to her sex lips would allow me to go. I sucked and bit all over my baby's neck, trying my best to heal her, to help her release Santana's murder. I hated that fuck nigga and felt he deserved everything she'd delivered to his punk ass. I wish I could have taken part in blowing his ass off of the map but loved her for doing it for the both of us.

"Uhhhhh, Bentley! I hate him!" She leaned back into me as we moved onto our backs with my fingers going in and out of her. Her thighs were cocked wide.

"Fuck that nigga, boo. Fuck him! You did that for me! For us. If he'd a still been here then I would not. Is that what you want? Huh? Huh? Huh?" My fingers worked over time.

"Aw. Aw. No-baby. Aw. No-baybee-yuh. Baby, I'm cumming. I'm cumming!"

I slid off of the bed and got between her legs, and held her pussy lips wide open. "Say fuck that nigga! Say it, baby!" I trapped her jewel and sucked.

She grabbed the sides of my head and held it, riding my face as fast as she could. "Uh! Fuck you. Shit!" More riding. "Fuck you, Santana! You tried. Aw, Bentley. You tried to kill my hubby. You tried."

I was sucking and slurping, licking up and down her slit, rubbing my nose all in it, then trapping her pearl all over again. Her juices ran down my neck, and along my chest. The feel of them sent chills through me. Made me wanna kill something for her. I sucked that pussy until she collapsed and fell back to sleep. I cuddled up behind my baby and held her. Soon, the remorse would pass. I just had to get her heart to turn colder.

***

The next night we sat around waiting for Guns to hit me up. It seemed that we were in every news outlet, and social media was going crazy calling us the modern-day *Natural Born Killers*. Some of the comments were almost comical. I honestly didn't give a fuck about none of that. I just wanted together the hell off of the East Coast and if at all possible, out of the United States altogether. I wanted Jade all to myself. I wanted us to start a new life where we ain't have to constantly look over our shoulders every second of every day.

Jade was curled on her side, playing with her phone when suddenly she sat up, looking down at it. "Oh, my God."

I finished lining myself up with the hair clippers. Just because we were on the run didn't mean I was supposed to let myself go. My waves were thick and all over my head in a nice pattern. I finished and cut the clippers off, looked at her through the mirror in the motel room. "What's good?"

"My favorite cousin, Fendi, just came on to Facebook. She's inquiring about me."

I shrugged my shoulders. "And?"

"And nothing, I was surprised that's all." She scrolled down the phone, and started to bite on her index fingernail.

"Jade, stop doing that shit. You know I don't like when your nails look all jacked up. Turn that phone off for a minute," I ordered. "Come over her and line me up in the back."

She did some more punching on her phone, and then slid off the bed. She grabbed the clippers, turning them on. "You making a lot of demands, hubby. Damn."

I smiled. "Shut up and get me right. I know the first thing we gotta do when we get where we going is to get your dreads re-twisted. Then handle them fingers and toes. You know you gotta keep them up to par." Jade had real pretty fingers and toes. They were the perfect shade of caramel brown. The knuckles on her fingers were slightly darker and that made them look even more precious to me. All around the board she was my perfect match.

"These aren't locked. My father was trying to make me, but they aren't. When we get to where we're going, I want to take them down and let my natural hair flow. It's nice and long and I think it's pretty. These dreads are like prison bars to me. I can't wait to release them."

There was a knock on the door of the motel. Jade dropped the clippers, and her and I both dashed and grabbed our guns, cocking them. She knelt on the side of the door and I put my back to the wall, to the left of the door. Pulled the curtain back just a tad and peeked out of the window.

Guns stood in front of it with his skull cap pulled low just above his eyes. He scanned the scene. Frowned, and started to knock again, this time more forcefully.

Jade whispered up to me, "Who is it, baby?" She climbed to a squat. Her pretty eyes lowered.

"Guns. I don't see nobody else." I stepped in front of the door. "Yo, who is it?"

"Guns, nigga. Damn, open the door, it's cold as hell out here."

I opened the door and pulled him inside. Stuck my head out and looked around, before closing the door after confirming that nothing looked out of the ordinary.

He mugged the both of us after the door closed and fixed his clothes. "Damn, y'all look like y'all ready to go to war. That's what's good. I come bearing good news." He pulled out a small bag and sat down on the edge of the bed.

Chapter 17

Jade

Guns held his phone and snapped my picture for the eighth time. "Okay, one should do it. I got every angle that I need. These cards gon come out real nice. Shorty work at the DMV, so she know what she doing. My other lil bitch a supervisor at the Social Security office, so she plugged too. Long story short, y'all are in good hands. I should have these back to you in a few days. In the meantime and in between times, Bentley, that mission has been supplemented for another one. And it's an urgent type of thing. Urgent, meaning tomorrow night. Since shorty seem like she a rider, she should probably roll out wit you, because you gon need a bitch by your side. I could supply you with my lil red ho from the projects, but I don't know how your shorty gon feel about that. Nah mean?" Guns put his phone away. Pulled out a small knot of hundreds, and tossed it to Bentley. "That five more gees."

Bentley caught it, and looked it over. "Blood, don't refer to or call my wife a bitch again. You got me? That's my queen. Not one of them punk-ass project bitches. Honor me on that, Blood. Aiight?" Bentley snapped. I could tell he was getting real heated. He was tired of mafuckas disrespecting me, as he should have been.

Guns held up his hands. "Look, my bad, Jade. I ain't mean to call you a bitch. It's just that a nigga been talking like this for so long. Every bitch is a bitch to me. But, I see what the homie mean, so I apologize." Messing with Guns, that was the probably the best apology we could look for. But, I felt nothing. Dudes had it bad, calling females out of their names anyway.

I rolled my eyes and turned my back to him. Picked up my phone and got on social media. I wanted to see if my cousin had hit me back up.

Bentley sat on the bed and looked over at Guns. "What's good wit this new mission?"

Guns cleared his throat. "You gon have to buck this Blanco nigga down at his Super Bowl party over in Newark. Gotta make a big splash too, that's the order. He just moved up here from Miami a few weeks back and trying to take over the flow of shit that's coming in from overseas. Slapping all kinds of taxes on the imported China White and everything. Trying to do the same bullying shit up here that he did down there, but that ain't happening. Mafuckas calling for his head already and since they already paid you for a mission that you was supposed to handle a few days ago, a mission that I wound up taking care of you, just gon have to show yo ass wit this one. It should be a hop, skip and a jump."

Bentley tossed the money back to him. "I'm good. I'ma give them niggas all their bread back and leave it at that. I got enough murders under my belt. Yo, just get them cards right so me and my Earth can break this seal of the States. Ain't shit here for us no more."

Guns stood up and mugged him. "Bruh, that ain't how this shit work. You've already entered into a contract with these niggas. You can't go backward now. You do that shit and my life is on the line, along with my integrity. Two things I ain't willing to risk losing, all because of you having a change of heart."

Bentley stood up and shrugged his shoulders. "Nigga, I don't give a fuck what you ain't trying to risk losing. I said what I said. It sounds like you setting me up for a death wish stunt. If this nigga was calling shots back in Miami, he gotta be plugged. The last thing I need is a bunch of mob niggas coming at my head, and all for what, a few bands? Nigga, yeah right."

Bentley walked to the door and got ready to open it. "Anything else you need, potna?"

Guns stood quiet. "Yo kid, you ain't finna do this to me. I'm connecting the dots all around the board, including this one. Now, I already filled in one blank for you, because you were out of town fucking wit Santana. Whatever bidness you two had ain't got shit to do wit me. But, before you left Jersey, you had a prior obligation. An obligation that I wound up fulfilling because I knew you was headed out there to fuck wit him. But, now you're back. I said I was gon call you or get in touch wit you when a mission came through, and here I am. Go handle that bidness tomorrow night."

Bentley sucked his teeth. "Nah, son, I'ma pass on this one. Besides, how the fuck am I supposed to get into this nigga's Super Bowl party anyway? If he slanging yay like I think he is, then he gon have security out the ass. I smoke him, who's to say they ain't gon smoke me?"

Guns ran his hand over his dreads. "That's why you gotta bring shorty wit you, kid, so she can watch your back. I mean, it's gon be niggas on deck that are up on the fact he's about to get hit. But still, you could never be too careful. As far as how you're getting into the party, you'll have an invitation with a plus one. That's why I said that it's important for you to have a female on hand with you. It'll make you look normal, and not only can she watch your back, but if she's a goon like Jade, then you can expect her to pop that cannon for you. They gon have a metal detector at this party, but I'ma have another lil bitch that's down for the cause already in place. She gon give both of y'all the tools you need to pull this shit off. It'll be smart to corner this nigga somewhere and blast his bitch ass. I know he make frequent trips to the bathroom for whatever reason, so maybe you can catch him in there and put that metal to him. I don't know how you gon do your thing, but clearly you ain't new to this shit. Just make it happen. You'll have everything you need to do what you have to."

Bentley nodded his head. "Aiight, give me an hour or so to talk that over with my woman and I'll be at you. It ain't just about me no more."

Guns curled his lip. "Yeah, well that's cool, but I'm letting you know right now that ain't shit moving with dem cards and passports until you hold your end as a man. I stuck my neck out for you. The least you can do is hold up yours." He grabbed the handle of the door and opened it. Glanced back at Bentley one time and then me. "I'm the ticket to you mafuckas breaking free. I'm the last one you should try and get over on." He tossed the roll of money back on the bed next to me, before leaving out and slamming the door behind him.

Bentley lowered his head. "Damn. What you think ma?"

I had my phone on the side of me with my head lowered, rubbing my temples. "When does it end, Bentley? When does all of this killing, and robbing, blood shedding end? I don't know how much more of it that I can really take." It felt like I had a pounding headache. Every time I opened my eyes the room seemed to be spinning. My stomach felt weird as well.

He slid his arm around my back, then hugged me to him. "If you don't want me to do it, baby, I won't. We got two hunnit gees, plus what he just gave us. We can go right now tonight. Just drive as far away from New York as we can. It's all about what you wanna do. I'm living for you right now. That's my word."

I was feeling too sick to respond, slid out of his embrace on wobbly legs. "Bentley, I don't feel so good. Seriously. I feel like I'm about to die." I jumped from the bed and ran into the bathroom as fast as I could. Got to the toilet and knelt in front of it, after flipping the lid up and purging my guts, I got to throwing up everything that I'd eaten.

Bentley rushed into the bathroom and pulled my hair out of my face, held it for me. "Damn, baby. Maybe it's that Chinese food from China Gardens. You think it disagreed with your stomach?" he asked, rubbing my back.

I couldn't think. All I wanted to do was to throw up as much as I could so I could feel better. My head was spinning worse than ever. I held the sides of the cool porcelain and tried to catch my breath. "I don't know, baby. I just got to feeling funny as of yesterday morning. Then all day today it's been crazy. Finally, I could hold it down anymore. I needed to get whatever bug that is in me out," I rasped.

He wiped my lips with his thumbs, then kissed me right on them. Grabbed a warm cloth, and ran it along the side of my face, and mouth. Flushed the toilet. "It's gon be okay, Jade. I got you. I got you." He picked me up and carried me into the bedroom, and laid me down slowly. "My baby. I got you, boo. Now, I don't want you to freak out, baby, but listen to me. Can you do that?" He fixed the pillow under my head and rushed into the bathroom. Wet the towel with cool water and placed it on my forehead.

"What were you finna say, baby? I think I'm about to throw up again." I sat up.

He rubbed my face and kissed my lips. "Baby, when was your last period?"

My heart skipped two beats. I was ready to lose my mind. My period. Damn. In the midst of our crazy lifestyle, I'd forgotten all about my period. I sat there and tried to remember the last one I'd had, and for the life of me could not. I started to shake.

Bentley knelt in front of me. "Goddess, I think you might be pregnant. And if that is the case, we gotta get the fuck out of the United States, like ASAP. Now, the only way we're going to be able to do that is if we hit this last lick for Guns, so we can get those identification cards, and passports. Ain't no other way."

I rushed out of the way and back to the bathroom, purging again. This time it was mostly dry heaves. A lot of gagging. Bentley was right by my side, holding my hair out of the way. His lips pressed to the back of neck. "I wish I could throw up for you, baby. Wish you didn't have to go at this alone."

I finished and once again, he kissed my lips. Pulled me into his big arms and we curled up on the bathroom floor. "I can't be pregnant, baby. We got so much to figure out. We don't know if we'll be here tomorrow. How are we going to raise or even prepare to raise a child?" I asked, feeling so dizzy.

"Long as we're together, we can do anything, you and I. There is nothing that this world can throw at us."

"We gotta put on Jehovah's full armor, Bentley. We need it so bad right now, baby."

He kissed my cheek. Rubbed up and down my thigh. "What's that?"

I swallowed my spit. My mouth was super dry. My voice raspy. "The armor of God, Bentley. The helmet of salvation. The breastplate of righteousness, and the shield of faith so that we can fight off all of the fiery darts of the evil one. The belt of truth, and we ask that he shods our feet, with the preparation for the gospel of peace, and for the sword of the spirit which is Jehovah's word."

"Baby, I don't know what any of that means but if you think we need it, then pray for us to have it."

I shook my head. "You're the head now, Bentley. You are Christ, and I am your church, baby. You have to pray. You

148

have to pray so our family can be covered. If it is a family that Jehovah is giving us. Do you hear me, baby?"

He moved my locks out of the way and kissed my cheek, before laying his against mine. "I'll do whatever it takes, baby. If you want me to pray I will. I'll pray for us every day and every now. But, just chill, ma. Take it easy. Please. We'll figure everything out if you do."

***

That night, I taught Bentley how to pray. He allowed me to read the scriptures to him, and he listened attentively and asked questions whenever he felt confused. I felt good doing this with him. For me, it was a connection much deeper than sex. And don't get me wrong, his sex game was on fire. But to sit there with my husband and be able to study the Bible while we hugged up with each other seemed magical to me. His words started to resonate in my mind, and when I edited them in just the slightest, they made sense to me. We could definitely do anything as long as we had the covering of God, and then each other. The further we studied, the deeper I fell in love with him. He became my truth.

Things were also confirmed that night. After Bentley came back from the drug store with four pregnancy tests of four different brands, it was determined that I was in fact, pregnant. That scared me more than the nightmares from Santana's murder.

Bentley paced back and forth with two guns in his hand. "Yo, all I know is these pistols, Jade. These pistols, that dope and stealing cars. How the hell am I gon raise a kid? Yo, I don't even like a nigga looking at you. I'm always paranoid about something bad happening to my rib, yo, if you give me a kid that came from your body and us mixed together. Man,

I'll be bucking stuff down all day on my super overprotective shit. Yo, and where am I gon work? Shorties are expensive as hell. Then, I gotta keep you rocking the latest. You're way too fine to be rocking anything less than that. Yo, what a life." He smiled and shook his head, then started to frown. "I'll never fail you though. Not my Jade. Not my rib."

I couldn't help giggling just watching him talk to himself. My hubby was really going through it. Overthinking, and envisioning what the future was going to look like, when most men would have been preparing to hit the road to find an easier situation. Man, I loved him. He was created for me and only me. I truly felt that. "Baby, come here," I ordered, holding my hands out to him after standing up.

He stopped mid pace and rushed to me. "What's the matter, baby? You need me to go the store to buy your cravings?"

Now this had me tickled pink. How in the hell was this boy about to go to the store to buy my craving? I laughed out loud, while he looked into my face confused. I rubbed the side of his face with tenderness. "Baby, we're going to be okay. We got this. Why don't you simply hold me for the night, and I can explain to you some of the things that you can look forward to now that I am pregnant. Starting with you buying my cravings?" I smiled.

Chapter 18

Bentley

"Nigga, just look at these bitches. I told you my girls were going to do their thing, didn't I? Look at 'em, they look better than professional, and the numbers on the cards register up too. Y'all are good to go. I mean, after you handle this bidness with Blanco," Gums said, standing up and pouring himself a shot of Hennessy. It was nine in the morning. I didn't know how he could jump out of the bed, and get to drinking right away like he was. But, that was something else that I'd noticed about thirty other people doing on my way into the Peter McGuire Projects and on the way up to his apartment. I guess to be able come to grips with the reality of living in the projects. You had to get started bright and early on numbing your brain.

Jade looked the cards over, and smiled, holding on to my right arm, with her chin resting on my shoulder. "Dang, these do look just like us though. But why you shoot for the name Eden Checkol? That make me sound like an old white woman," she added, scrunching her nose.

"Shid, that sound better than Rufus Checkol. My name sound like an old ass man," I said, looking over my social security card, new identification cards, and papers.

Guns wiped his mouth and burped. "And both of them sound better than your real names, because your real names are on fire. And if you keep them, these white folks gon set y'all ass on fire too. Word up. Now, these will definitely get you out of the country, and to one of them non-extraditing countries below the border. Can a nigga get a thank you? A, that's love, a something? Damn." He looked us over offended.

I stood up and gave him a half-hug, pat his back. "Good looking, bruh. On some real shit, you looked out and we appreciate that. You know we on fire. We gotta get a move on real fast, so go ahead and give us the lowdown on this move." I slid beside Jade and helped her to rest her head on my shoulder. This was another morning where she had felt a bit under the weather. Had thrown up twice already at Guns' crib.

"Good looking too, Guns. You know, on the cards and stuff," Jade said, just above a whisper.

"Don't mention it. You just make sure you watch my nigga back on this move. You do that and consider us even." Guns sat down, and picked up a blunt, sparking it. "Aiight, now to this move. It's real simple really. You and your lady are going to enter into the party just like the other people that were invited. It's a Super Bowl party, so y'all just enjoy yourselves for a few hours, and the whole while, keep your eyes peeled for Blanco, and on Blanco. Like I told you before, he gon be making frequent trips to the bathroom. He'll probably use the one that is upstairs from the party. You catch him there and lace his ass. The fellas want as much of the clip emptied into his face as possible. He stepping on a lot of cats' toes. Mafuckas want his blood shed. Nah mean. The better a job you do, the better it makes me look. I'm just keeping it one hunnit. Anyway, after you lace this punk, you can be on your way. Like I said before, the guns will be silenced. Nine millimeters. My bitch on the inside that's working as a waitress is gon hand them to y'all when the time is right. She'll be dark-skinned with long, flowing dreadlocks. Real pretty. Might ask you into the bathroom, Jade. I don't know yet."

"Guns, if you got everything figured out to a science like this, why in the hell do you need me and my husband to do this? Why you can't have any ol' run of the mill crackhead to

Life of Sin 2

do it?" Jade asked, taking two deep breaths directly after asking the question.

I rubbed her back and looked over to Guns for his response. "You're okay, baby?"

She nodded. "Yeah, just a bit nauseous. I'll be alright though."

Guns gave her one of those, "you're overstepping your bounds" looks. Was about to say something and caught himself. Wound up smiling. "I don't need no crack head to do it. I got y'all. Bedsides, a deal is a deal. This just what it is. Aight?" He got off of the couch and opened his refrigerator. Took out a carton of eggs. Grabbed a loaf of bread off the top of the refrigerator, then got to washing his hands. "Yo, my word, I'm about to whip up my mother's famous Camden French toast, and you two are going to eat. Especially you, Jade. You being pregnant and all. I'ma bless you with these cheese omelets and all that shit too. If it's one thing the god can do, that's cook. Word. So, I'ma get you right. I got you."

I grew offended and jealous right away. "Nigga, hold on, I don't need you trying to get her right. I got that. This me right here. I got her." I wrapped my arm more securely around Jade. I ain't want nobody doing shit for her if I could do it myself, especially not no nigga. I didn't give a fuck who they was. That didn't make no difference.

"Be smooth, Bentley, damn. Nigga, I ain't pushing up on ya rib. I'm saying this in a brotherly way. I'm cooking for you too. That means I got you too."

Jade laid her head under my neck and rubbed my right bicep. "Guns, how did you know that I was pregnant? Ain't nobody said nothing about that."

"Your mannerisms, ma. Yo, you done threw up a few times already. Then the homie super overprotective of you right now. In order to survive in this jungle, you gotta pick up

153

all telltale signs. He ain't stopped groping you or kissing you yet. The homie head over heels right now in love and protection. But, that's what's up though, because out of me, him, and Santana, Bentley used to be the biggest player. I'm talking bad bitches. All the time. And mostly Spanish. He had a thing for them. Was a lil bit of a ho. But, I can tell you done cast that spell on him that only a sista could have. That's what's really good though. I'm wishing y'all the best." He was all around the kitchen like he knew what he was doing. "So, y'all gon eat or not?"

"I am," Jade replied. "It's smelling good already. I most definitely am. Yo, Guns, what kind of sausages are you using?"

He reached into the refrigerator and pulled out a pound of Tennessee Pride sausages. "Swine, my brother?" Then he was cracking up.

I kissed Jade's forehead and rubbed her soft beautiful face. "I love you, boo. You hear me? I'd kill a nigga for you with no hesitation. You're my baby. Both of you." I rubbed her li'l flat stomach, even snuck my hand under her shirt so I could feel her, skin on skin. I was growing crazier over her by the hour. I still couldn't believe she was having my shorty. Our child. Man, life was crazy.

She maneuvered her head until our lips were sucking on each other's, kissed me long and hard holding the side of my face, her tongue dancing and gliding along the length of mine. I felt my piece sticking up. We needed to chill or I was about to go in her right there in Gun's living room.

I broke our embraces and she laid her head back on my shoulder. "Guns, what time this party kick off, my nigga? Or better yet, what time should we be there?"

"Three o'clock. That's what time y'all gon stroll through. Everything will be set in place at that time. That's about four hours and some change from now." I could hear him cracking an egg over the skillet. The sizzling, and then the scent of the other food that he'd cooked rose into the air. Made my stomach growl like an angry bear protecting its cub.

Jade's stomach was roaring as well. More than once, I saw her sniff with her nose in the direction of the kitchen. "Dang, he gotta hurry up." Her phone buzzed. She looked at the face and sat on the edge of the couch. "Oh, my God, it's my mother reaching out to me. How in the hell did she get my contact information?" she said out loud and stood up with the phone.

I stood up with her. "What you finna do?" I asked.

She shrugged her shoulders. "I don't know. What should I do?" She looked at the face again.

"Yo, Guns, we about to use your bathroom, kid, we'll be right out," I hollered.

He was in the kitchen doing his thing now. Singing a song to himself. He waved us off and kept handling his bidness.

After the bathroom door closed. Jade took a deep breath and Facetimed with her mother. Before her mother even said a word, she was in tears. "Mama, oh my God, how are you doing?" she asked, shaking.

Jade's mother smiled. "I'm good, baby. How are you?"

Jade shook her head. "Scared. Wondering how you could tell them it was me that did that to Daddy when you know I could never do such a thing. I hit him with the lamp, but I never stabbed him, Mama and you know I didn't. How could you do that?"

Her mother sighed. "Jade, I know you did it to protect me. It's okay. I forgive you, baby. But, you need to turn yourself in. You and that boy."

Jade was crying hard now. "Where are the twins? Let me talk too, or see Ashley and Ashland. Please."

Her mother shook her head. "I ain't got 'em back yet, but when I do, you can surely see them. Jade, where are you, baby? I wanna come get you."

Now my paranoia kicked all the way in. Something didn't feel right. "Hang up, baby. It's a trap," I ordered her.

"Jade? Who is that? Is that that boy? That murderer?" she asked.

"Mama, when will you have the twins back? I miss them so much." She squeezed her eyes together and began to sob.

"Hang up the phone, Jade. Now, ma."

"Jade? Where are you? Mama wanna come get you. I need to tell you that—"

I snatched the phone out of her hand and threw it as hard as I could into the hard porcelain tub, shattering it into a hundred pieces. Then picked up as many pieces as I could and dumped them into the toilet, flushing.

Jade fell to her knees sobbing, rocking back and forth on them. "I miss my sisters, Bentley. I miss my sisters so, so much. It's not fair. It's just not," she cried.

I fell to the floor and pulled her into my arms, holding her as tight as I could. "It's okay, baby. It's okay. I got you now. I got you."

It took us thirty minutes to get ourselves together after the phone call. When we got back into the kitchen, Guns had the table laid out with a breakfast fit for champions. There was a platter of cheese omelets. One of sausage patties and another one for the Camden French toast that he'd made. A big jug of Mr. Pure orange juice, and he was stirring grits. I pulled Jade's chair out for her and waited until she sat down in it.

"Damn, you got my nigga pulling chairs out for you and shit. Your fine ass took every ounce of his G-card. What y'all think, this the fifties a something?" he joked, getting our plates together.

156

"He doing what a man is supposed to, Guns. This is how a man treats a queen when he loves her." She kissed my cheeks and took a deep breath. Her eyes were still red.

"Oh yeah? Well, let me show you how a nigga treat a bitch he just fucking. Shorty! Shorty, get yo yella ass out here before you starve. Bring you and that chocolate bitch so y'all can eat," he hollered toward the back of the small apartment.

Jade shook her head. "I guess." Grabbed her plate and picked up the utensils.

The two females came out of the back room dressed in just a pair of booty shorts, and tight tank tops that exposed the fact that they were braless. Their nipples poked against the material. They each walked into the kitchen and kissed Guns on his cheeks, before sitting at the table with both me and Jade.

Jade rolled her eyes and took my hand, praying over our food. After she finished, she started to chow down, mugging the girls every so often, turning her nose up.

The yella girl couldn't take her eyes off of me, neither could the dark-skinned sista. They would eat some of their food, and then whisper to each other. Laugh, and keep on eating. I could tell that they were very immature for their age, especially if they were supposed to be eighteen.

Finally Jade slapped her hand on the table. "Hey. You bitches need to look somewhere else, because looking at him a get you kilt, quick. You got that?" she asked, mugging them with deathly hatred.

The dark-skinned girl curled her lip, then sucked her teeth loudly. "Bitch, if you don't want nobody looking at your man, then he shouldn't be so fucking fine. Look at how his waves popping and he got them deep ass dimples. I'll fuck him right here and right now in front of yo ass. Bitch, this is the McGuires. Don't nobody know you."

With lightning speed, Jade reached across the table and grabbed a handful of her hair, used it to slam her face in the plate of Camden French toast two times. Flipped the whole table, and straddled her hitting her with blow after blow. "Punk. Bitch. This Red Hook. This Brooklyn. This. Is. My. Husband. Mine."

The yella broad got up and ran to the room. Me and Guns stood back while Jade did her thing. The rules of the projects said that we were to let them finish their fight without intervening. The rules were the same in New York, as they were in Camden, New Jersey.

When Jade had knocked the girl out, she stood up, and looked down on her, then over to me. "Bentley, next time you better check these hood rats before it comes to this. You already know this ain't a game." She looked at her ring. "Damn, now I gotta wash her blood out of this thing." She shook her head.

Gun nodded his head. "Yeah, nigga, on my blood I would have wifed her too. Damn, she a rider!" He jumped up excitedly.

Chapter 19

Jade

Bentley stepped up to the big bouncer and handed him the silver edged piece of paper that went for an invitation. The big Black man that stood about six feet eleven inches tall, and weighed every bit of three hundred plus pounds, snatched the invitation out of his hand and looked him over, before scanning the paperwork. "Names?" he growled, sounding like a big ass Gorilla.

"Mr. and Mrs. Checkol. We were invited by Blanco himself as you can see right there on the invitation."

He grunted. "Yeah, I see that. Nigga, I can read." He pulled out a tablet and scrolled down the screen until he located our names. "Aw right, Mr. and Mrs. Checkol. You're good to go. He reached into a box that was on the side of him and lulled out gold bracelets, clicking them onto our right wrists. "Aw right. Hold on." Took a scanning wand and trailed them up and down both myself and Bentley. After confirming we were without weapons, we walked through a metal detector and into the big white mansion.

Bentley stopped short of the threshold and dusted off his Gucci suit, adjusting the cuff links. He looked like a handsome boss, and smelled just as good, cocked his arm for me to take it, which I did. "Jade, I just gotta let you know you killing that Gucci skirt dress ma. Word up. It's clinging to every one of your curves. Yo, you looking like Bathsheba. Enticing me in every kind of way." He flirted, trying to show me the lesson I'd recently taught him from the Bible was still fresh on his brain. It was attractive. To teach your man something and he actually picked the most spontaneous ways to show you that he'd paid attention was just everything for me.

"Thank you, baby, and you looking mighty fine yourself. Make me feel good to have such a husband."

He flashed his dimples. Un-huh." He scanned the party. "Dang. I'm glad we did get fresh first. Everybody in here look like they fitted. All I'm seeing is designer shit."

The party seemed to already be going off without a hitch. There were people all in the middle of the floor, dancing to some kind of Spanish music that I was unfamiliar with. And they were getting it in too. The mansion was packed with waitresses and waiters roaming about offering drinks and snacks. There were two long tables filled up with all kinds of food and drinks. Then another one reserved strictly for liquor. All of them had servers behind them. I was impressed. "Dang, Bentley, this is a party. They going hard."

He slid his arm around my lower back. "Don't worry, boo, when we get to where we going I'ma throw you a birthday party that's gon crush this one. You already know I gotta spoil my baby. Ain't that right."

"I don't know, baby. Looking around it seem like you gon have your work cut out for you. I'd fall back on hyping that birthday party up," I teased.

He shot me a look. Then laughed. "Aw okay. Yeah we'll see. Come on, let's blend in." Took my hand and led me to the dance floor.

I slid my arms around his neck. Looked into his caramel eyes and exhaled. Damn, he was fine, with those thick eyebrows, long eyelashes, and his deep dimples that appeared every time he said a word. If I never saw him get down in the streets, I would have never understood how a man so fine could survive in the jungles we'd come from. Red Hook was crazy.

"Yo, what time bruh say you supposed to meet up with this dark-skinned chick to get them burners?" he asked, missing my cheek and sliding his hands down to my butt, rubbing all over it, cuffing it just a bit, before letting it go.

I got tingles. Every time he touched me, I got them and I didn't that would ever change. "He said closer to five, right around kickoff time. That way everybody would be engrossed in the big game." As I said this, about ten movers came, rolling big flat screened televisions across the dance floor, headed toward the front of the mansion. Each one had on a blue Best Buy jackets. Whoever this Blanco stud was, he was most definitely going all out for this party. I wondered what his obsession was with the Super Bowl.

Hell, I had a brief understanding of what it was myself. I didn't really like football. Every time it came across the screen in our apartment, my father would be set in front of the screen drinking heavily. As soon as the game ended, that is when the arguing, fighting, and beatings began. Over the years, I'd grown to hate football.

"Aw that's cool. Well, in the meantime, we need to keep an eye out for this Blanco nigga. You remember how he look from the photos Guns showed us, right?"

I nodded and hugged up to him. "Yeah, baby. We're good. We just hon' handle our business and get out if here hopefully before the game is over. Then we can grab our money, identifications, and get the hell out of here."

He kissed my neck. "Yeah, it's gone be me and you, Jade. Just me and my missus. Well, that is until our lil one come. Still can't believe you're pregnant. I feel like the luckiest man in the world. I feel blessed."

"There you go, baby. Luck ain't got nothing to do with none of this. Everything is a blessing from Jehovah. Look at you learning how you learning. Making me feel some type of way. Give me those lips." I held his face and kissed his thick lips. Licked them and sucked them into my mouth. Stepped forward into his muscular body, and felt his manhood pressed up against me. It felt so good. He felt so good. I loved this man.

He broke our kiss and took my hand. "Come on, baby. Let's get you a few of these snacks. I need you to keep stuffing that face. I want a big fat baby. One that look just like you."

I yanked my hand away from him. "Boy, you tryna say I'm fat?" I asked, feeling a bit insecure. I knew I was set to blow all the way up while I was pregnant, so if he thought I was already fat, then he'd be in for a big surprise six or so months down the road.

"Hell n'all, and even if you were, I'd be obsessed wit you. Yo, I'm just saying I want our baby to be nice and healthy, and hopefully he or she looks just like you. My wife is a dime. Ain't no flex about that. Now come on, let's get you fed."

We wound up at the snack table where Bentley loaded up my plate with all kinds of goodies. Then we stepped away and took a seat right off of the veranda. I picked over the food and kept my eyes peeled for Blanco. So far, we'd had yet to spot him.

Bentley scanned the entire room, before looking back over to me. "Baby, after this, me and you gon live us a good life where we ain't gotta be doing all of this killing. We ain't gon be on the run, or have to constantly look over our shoulder. That's why we gotta get out of this country. So I can spoil you like I'm supposed to. I'ma spoil yo fine ass rotten. You got my word on that." He kissed my cheek again, tossing a stick of gum into his mouth. "Do you believe me?"

I nodded. "Of course I do, baby. I believe every word that's coming out of your mouth. But, I see we gon have to work on that tongue a lil bit."

162

"Yo, we can go in the bathroom and you can work on my tongue right now. Word up. I need to taste my wife anyway." I shook my head. "Boy. I'm talking about your language. Your speech. You curse too much. I'm trying to build myself a kingdom man. And, that tongue is the first thing we'll have to conquer. The Bible says you're head of our family, which means Jehovah inspects your tongue daily because you have to pray over us and our child when it gets here. We have to clean up that tongue so our family can be filled with blessings instead of curses. There is life and death in the power of your tongue, baby."

He lowered his head. "Dang baby. Let's just take a breather on all that stuff for a lil while. You know I'm a street nigga. I'm learning, and am willing to learn, but I ain't there yet. Just let me cruise. You can't cleanse a killa in one week."

"I know, baby. You're right. But ultimately, that's my goal. We're about to be parents now. A lot of things have to change. But for now, you're okay."

"So, I can cuss and you ain't gon feel no type of way?" he asked, then stood up.

"Yeah, baby, you can cuss. Just—"

He nodded his head. "Look, that gotta be that nigga Blanco right there."

A sharply dressed, handsome Spanish man walked through the front door with two body guards walking closely behind him. He puffed on a cigar in one hand and in the other used a cane to lean on.

Bentley pulled out his phone and looked over the picture of Blanco that was on it. I did the same thing, and sure enough it was him alright. The tattoo of the words and numbers MS-13 were in big bold lines along his neck.

"Hell yeah, that's his bitch ass. How the fuck we finna get close to him when he got two bodyguards walking closely behind him like that?" Bentley asked, frowning. "I might wind up smoking more than just that nigga. Shit."

"I don't know. Guns said he goes to the bathroom a lot, so maybe that's how. Otherwise you might be right. We might have to get our hands a lot dirtier than we previously imagined. I'm not ready for no more nightmares." I watched Blanco walk across the room giving out hugs. As he traveled, all of the people's eyes seemed to follow him as if he were some sort of celebrity. He looked to be about thirty or so years of age. I wondered why he used a cane to get around.

As my eyes were pinned on him, one of the waitresses came from the back of the mansion and walked up to me with a platter of drinks. "Excuse me, ma'am, may I interest you in one of our variety of cocktails?" she asked. Her dark skin looked as smooth as a newborn baby's. Her eyes were gray. Her short dreads were neatly twisted.

"No thank you. Maybe later," I said, dismissing her as polite as possible. My focus was on Blanco. I wanted us to handle him and get on with our lives. Had a lot more work yo do on Bentley before he was transformed into the kingdom husband that I knew he could become.

She smiled and leaned into me. "Jade, follow me. I need to holler at you right quick." She walked toward the back of the house, and it was then that I realized who she was.

I nudged Bentley. "Baby, that's her. I gotta go get our weapons. Meet me in the bathroom. Wherever that is. I'll have her show me." I kissed his lips and headed in the direction of the dark-skinned sista.

***

164

She knelt down in the small room and pulled a duffle bag from under the bed. Unzipped it and tossed me two chrome pistols that had silencers attached to their barrels. "Look, y'all gon have about twenty minutes to get this job done. Blanco's people from Brazil will be here in like thirty, because there is a deal going down during this party. They are crazy about him and have so much security it'll blow your mind. Currently, he's using replacement security that is on board with his assassination. Do what you have to and be ghost. Rita is going to trick him into going upstairs. That's where you should make your move. The bathroom is down the hall and to the right. I'm out of here." She opened the door and peeked out of it, before slipping into the hallway.

I tucked the guns into my Gucci bag that she'd given me and eased down the hallway and met up with Bentley in the bathroom.

Chapter 20

Bentley

Time was ticking. And my heart was pounding in my chest. One last move and it was all over. We'd be scot free to start a new life outside of the country. The only person standing in the way of that was Blanco. As long as he had life inside of his body, our lives could not be put back to normal. So, he had to be dealt with.

I watched him wrap his arm around a small Spanish female. She whispered something in his ear that made him hold up one finger. A big dude walked over to him and whispered something in his other ear. This made him perk up. He scanned the expanse of the party, and his eyes seemed to stop on me and Jade, or maybe I was tripping. Then he continued to look over the people in the party, before the big goon walked away nodding his head. The Spanish female rubbed his chest and pulled him down so she could whisper into his ear again. Whatever she said to him caused him to laugh. He looked behind her and ran his hand over her ass, squeezed it and sucked his bottom lip. She took his hand and led him through the party. They made their way toward the stairs, right before the same big goon from a few seconds ago jogged to him and whispered into his ear.

This made him perk up. He frowned, and shook off the Spanish chick, just as the waiters came through, pushing carts that were filled with silver platters of all kinds of powders. Blanco headed to the front of the mansion, and out of sight. The Spanish chick stood with her arms crossed. Took out her phone and began to text on it like crazy.

Jade rubbernecked watching the event unfold just as I had. "Baby, something ain't right. I don't know what's going on, but something is most definitely wrong."

I felt the heavy pistol tucked in my waist band. I didn't know what was going on either, but as long as I was strapped, I felt like I was prepared for it. "Yeah, boo, you're right. Come on, let's blend into this party a li'l bit. We down to seven minutes before we gotta go kamikaze and smoke that nigga. Either way, he gotta inhale these slugs. He was the only one standing in the way of our new life. Fuck that." I was getting more and more irritated by the second. I wanted to be done. Gone. On the highway already. Headed toward the border.

Jade took my hand and we wound up on the dance floor grooving to a song by Alicia Keys. We danced about and got closer and closer to the area of where Blanco had disappeared. Once we were close enough, I was able to look down the hallway to see him and the big goon still locked in a deep conversation. Blanco's arms swung wildly through the air as he chewed the dude out. Then he was storming down the hallway taking big steps. Angry. I searched for the two men that acted as security for him from earlier. They were nowhere in sight.

"Baby, he coming this way. What do we do?" Jade asked, tensing up.

"Nothin, just keep dancing. We're good." I grabbed ahold of her soft ass and kneaded it like dough. Man, Jade was strapped. I still couldn't get over how perfect her body was to me, and I knew the baby would only make her even more stacked. I couldn't wait. The lust in me nearly caused me to lose my focus. I glanced at my watch and saw that we had literally on a few minutes until his crew from South America was set to show up.

The Spanish chick from earlier came and stepped in front of him. Ran her fingers through her long hair, and started to say something, before running her hands over his chest.

Blanco hugged her to him and palmed her ass much like I'd done Jade's. Whispered into her ear and laughed. Nodded his head toward the stairs.

She licked her juicy, red coated lips, and pulled him toward them. They made their way up the stairs, and I felt a sense of relief.

"That must be the chick that the sista was telling me about. She said he would lead her up the stairs. Let's wait a minute then we gon follow them." Jade said, mugging the pair. She looked so fuckin' sexy, looking all evil and shit.

"Fuck that. We gotta go hit dude ass now." I looked toward the front door as a group of Spanish men eased into the party. They were tatted up all over their faces, and necks. Instead of being casually dressed like everybody else, they wore plaid shirts and khakis pants. I saw this after they took their coats off and handed them to the help.

Jade's eyes got bucked as she looked them over. "Damn. They definitely look like they about that life. They waist look chunky too, baby. They must not have gone through the metal detector."

I peeped the same thing. Took her hand and headed toward the steps. "Come on."

We took them swiftly. Got to the top of the flight and heard the sounds of loud moaning already. "Damn, he ain't waste no time, did he?" I asked, looking down to Jade.

"He probably knew them dudes were on the way. Tryna hurry up and get him a quickie."

She slid the gun out of her bag and cocked it like I'd shown her.

I put some pep in my step. Rushed down the hallway, and stopped at the door I knew the pair was in. Looked Jade over and took the nine out of my waistband. Counted with my fingers, held up one, then two of them, and then the third. Turned the knob and pushed the door inward.

Blanco had the Spanish girl bent over the oak desk fucking her hard from the back with his pants around his ankles. His eyes were closed and he was breathing harder than a dog pulling a sled. When the Spanish female saw us, she screamed, "Just him, not me."

Blanco's eyes shot open. He frowned. "What are you doing up here, chico? The party is downstairs."

"Hurry, baby," Jade urged.

I raised the gun and fired four quick shots.

Zoop. Zoop. Zoop. Zoop.

The firearm jumped in my hand. Big sparks flew out of it, despite the silencer on the end of it. The room filled with the stench of burnt gun powder.

Blanco flew over the desk, and wound up on his back, bloodied. He struggled to get up. Breathing heavy. Cursing in Spanish. I rushed over to him and put three more into him at point-blank range, deading him. He lay in the middle of the floor, a big puddle of blood forming around his body.

The Spanish woman covered her head. I stopped in front of her ready to blast, when Jade grabbed my wrist. "N'all, baby. We're done now. Let's get the heck out of here. Give her a pass."

I mugged the broad and everything in my soul told me to ice her as well. But instead, I listened to my rib, and we jetted out of there. Hopped in the whip and stormed away from the scene before anybody became the wiser.

***

The next morning, I met up with Guns at a burger joint on 33rd Street in South Camden. He slid into the back of the whip and started up right away. "Nigga, yousa monster. Both of y'all. Damn, y'all handled ya bidness, and wit all of them Brazilian niggas there too. Y'all the truth, man. Word to my mother, y'all the truth." He handed me a small Crown Royal knapsack. "It got everything in there. The IDs, the social security cards. The passports. Yo, y'all have a nice life. Word up. Get the fuck outta the East Coast at the very least."

I turned around and smiled at him. "Yo, good looking, bruh. My word, you looked out. I owe you, kid, if there is ever anything, I can do for you once I settle, just let me know."

Jade turned and adjusted herself in her seat. Then she began to rifle through the Gucci bag the dark-skinned sista had given her, as if she'd lost something.

Guns laughed. "It's all good. But bruh, you know they already putting up a half million dollars on the heads of the mafuckas that kilt Blanco. That's crazy, ain't it? I mean, that shit just happened yesterday." He laughed again and looked out of the back window. Then back up to me.

"He musta been a major nigga, that's all," I said out loud. "Yo, but anyway, we about to embark on this journey, bruh, I'ma fuck wit you in a minute." I turned around and started the car.

Guns nodded and with lightning speed, upped a .40 Glock out of his waistband and slammed it into the back of my head so hard that I could feel it bust it. "Nigga, they want that ass dead or alive, and I ain't passing up on no half-million dollars for nobody. Not even for my dope fiend ass mother. Ain't nothin' personal. Forgive me, Dunn."

Boom. Boom.

To Be Continued...
Life of Sin 3
Coming Soon

Submission Guideline

Submit the first three chapters of your completed manuscript to ldpsubmissions@gmail.com, subject line: Your book's title. The manuscript must be in a .doc file and sent as an attachment. Document should be in Times New Roman, double spaced and in size 12 font. Also, provide your synopsis and full contact information. If sending multiple submissions, they must each be in a separate email.

Have a story but no way to send it electronically? You can still submit to LDP/Ca$h Presents. Send in the first three chapters, written or typed, of your completed manuscript to:

**LDP: Submissions Dept
Po Box 870494
Mesquite, Tx 75187**

DO NOT send original manuscript. Must be a duplicate.

Provide your synopsis and a cover letter containing your full contact information.

Thanks for considering LDP and Ca$h Presents.

Life of Sin 2

A HUSTLER'S DECEIT 3

KILL ZONE **II**

BAE BELONGS TO ME III

SOUL OF A MONSTER

By **Aryanna**

THE COST OF LOYALTY **III**

By **Kweli**

SHE FELL IN LOVE WITH A REAL ONE **II**

By **Tamara Butler**

RENEGADE BOYS **III**

By **Meesha**

CORRUPTED BY A GANGSTA **IV**

By **Destiny Skai**

A GANGSTER'S CODE **III**

By **J-Blunt**

KING OF NEW YORK V

RISE TO POWER III

COKE KINGS II

By **T.J. Edwards**

GORILLAZ IN THE BAY III

De'Kari

THE STREETS ARE CALLING II

Duquie Wilson

KINGPIN KILLAZ IV

STREET KINGS 2

PAID IN BLOOD 2

Hood Rich

T.J. & Jelissa

SINS OF A HUSTLA II
ASAD
TRIGGADALE II
Elijah R. Freeman
MARRIED TO A BOSS III
By Destiny Skai & Chris Green
KINGS OF THE GAME III
Playa Ray

<u>**Available Now**</u>
<u>RESTRAINING ORDER **I & II**</u>
By **CA$H & Coffee**
<u>LOVE KNOWS NO BOUNDARIES **I II & III**</u>
By **Coffee**
<u>RAISED AS A GOON I, II, III & IV</u>
<u>BRED BY THE SLUMS I, II, III</u>
<u>BLAST FOR ME I & II</u>
<u>ROTTEN TO THE CORE I III</u>
<u>A BRONX TALE I, II, III</u>
<u>DUFFEL BAG CARTEL I II</u>
By **Ghost**
<u>LAY IT DOWN **I & II**</u>
<u>LAST OF A DYING BREED</u>
<u>BLOOD STAINS OF A SHOTTA I & II</u>
By **Jamaica**
<u>LOYAL TO THE GAME</u>

LOYAL TO THE GAME II

LOYAL TO THE GAME III

LIFE OF SIN I, II

By **TJ & Jelissa**

BLOODY COMMAS I & II

SKI MASK CARTEL I II & III

KING OF NEW YORK I II,III IV

RISE TO POWER I II

COKE KINGS

By **T.J. Edwards**

IF LOVING HIM IS WRONG…I & II

LOVE ME EVEN WHEN IT HURTS I II

By **Jelissa**

WHEN THE STREETS CLAP BACK I & II III

By **Jibril Williams**

A DISTINGUISHED THUG STOLE MY HEART I II & III

LOVE SHOULDN'T HURT I II III

RENEGADE BOYS I & II

By **Meesha**

A GANGSTER'S CODE I &, II III

By **J-Blunt**

PUSH IT TO THE LIMIT

By **Bre' Hayes**

BLOOD OF A BOSS **I, II, III, IV, V**

By **Askari**

THE STREETS BLEED MURDER **I, II & III**

THE HEART OF A GANGSTA I II& III

177

T.J. & Jelissa

By **Jerry Jackson**
CUM FOR ME
CUM FOR ME 2
CUM FOR ME 3
CUM FOR ME 4
An **LDP Erotica Collaboration**
BRIDE OF A HUSTLA **I II & II**
THE FETTI GIRLS **I, II& III**
CORRUPTED BY A GANGSTA I, II & III
By **Destiny Skai**
WHEN A GOOD GIRL GOES BAD
By **Adrienne**
THE COST OF LOYALTY
By Kweli
A GANGSTER'S REVENGE **I II III & IV**
THE BOSS MAN'S DAUGHTERS
THE BOSS MAN'S DAUGHTERS II
THE BOSSMAN'S DAUGHTERS III
THE BOSSMAN'S DAUGHTERS IV
THE BOSS MAN'S DAUGHTERS **V**
A SAVAGE LOVE **I & II**
BAE BELONGS TO ME I II
A HUSTLER'S DECEIT I, II, III
WHAT BAD BITCHES DO I, II, III
By **Aryanna**
A KINGPIN'S AMBITON
A KINGPIN'S AMBITION **II**

178

I MURDER FOR THE DOUGH

By **Ambitious**

TRUE SAVAGE

TRUE SAVAGE II

TRUE SAVAGE **III**

TRUE SAVAGE **IV**

TRUE SAVAGE **V**

TRUE SAVAGE **VI**

By **Chris Green**

A DOPEBOY'S PRAYER

By **Eddie "Wolf" Lee**

THE KING CARTEL **I, II & III**

By **Frank Gresham**

THESE NIGGAS AIN'T LOYAL **I, II & III**

By **Nikki Tee**

GANGSTA SHYT **I II &III**

By **CATO**

THE ULTIMATE BETRAYAL

By **Phoenix**

BOSS'N UP **I , II & III**

By **Royal Nicole**

I LOVE YOU TO DEATH

By Destiny J

I RIDE FOR MY HITTA

I STILL RIDE FOR MY HITTA

By **Misty Holt**

LOVE & CHASIN' PAPER

T.J. & Jelissa

By **Qay Crockett**

TO DIE IN VAIN

SINS OF A HUSTLA

By **ASAD**

BROOKLYN HUSTLAZ

By **Boogsy Morina**

BROOKLYN ON LOCK I & II

By **Sonovia**

GANGSTA CITY

By **Teddy Duke**

A DRUG KING AND HIS DIAMOND I & II III

A DOPEMAN'S RICHES

HER MAN, MINE'S TOO I, II

CASH MONEY HO'S

By Nicole Goosby

TRAPHOUSE KING **I II & III**

KINGPIN KILLAZ I II III

STREET KINGS

PAID IN BLOOD

By **Hood Rich**

LIPSTICK KILLAH **I, II, III**

CRIME OF PASSION I & II

By **Mimi**

STEADY MOBBN' **I, II, III**

By **Marcellus Allen**

WHO SHOT YA **I, II**

Renta

GORILLAZ IN THE BAY **I II**

DE'KARI

TRIGGADALE

Elijah R. Freeman

GOD BLESS THE TRAPPERS I, II, III

THESE SCANDALOUS STREETS I, II, III

FEAR MY GANGSTA I, II, III

THESE STREETS DON'T LOVE NOBODY I, II

BURY ME A G I, II, III, IV, V

A GANGSTA'S EMPIRE I, II, III

Tranay Adams

THE STREETS ARE CALLING

Duquie Wilson

MARRIED TO A BOSS... I II

By Destiny Skai & Chris Green

KINGS OF THE GAME I II

Playa Ray

T.J. & Jelissa

BOOKS BY LDP'S CEO, CA$H

TRUST IN NO MAN
TRUST IN NO MAN 2
TRUST IN NO MAN 3
BONDED BY BLOOD
SHORTY GOT A THUG
THUGS CRY
THUGS CRY 2
THUGS CRY 3
TRUST NO BITCH
TRUST NO BITCH 2
TRUST NO BITCH 3
TIL MY CASKET DROPS
RESTRAINING ORDER
RESTRAINING ORDER 2
IN LOVE WITH A CONVICT

Coming Soon
BONDED BY BLOOD 2
BOW DOWN TO MY GANGSTA

Life of Sin 2